## DEATH ON THE SUPERSLAB

The renegade rig kept up the assault. The shooter was back now, the smaller automatic weapon in his hands again. Both rigs swerved across the roadway like snakes on hot coals.

Marc glanced out his window and saw the silhouette of the shooter when the guy raised the autogun to fire. "Here it comes."

A stream of flying death pellets slammed into the bullet resistant glass at Marc's head. The sophisticated transparent material survived the onslaught unscathed. The shooter's death slugs spent their energy harmlessly and slammed into the pavement below.

"Nice try, dickhead," Carl screamed. "Eat this." He touched off a three-round burst from the rotatable 20mm cannons in the front cowling of the Leeco rig. The barrage slammed into the Peterbilt and caused the front end to sail skyward into a thousand fiery fragments.

Bantam Books by Bob Ham

OVERLOAD #1: PERSONAL WAR
OVERLOAD #2: THE WRATH
OVERLOAD #3: HIGHWAY WARRIORS
OVERLOAD #4: TENNESSEE TERROR (Super Edition)
OVERLOAD #5: ATLANTA BURN
OVERLOAD #6: NEBRASKA NIGHTMARE
OVERLOAD #7: ROLLING VENGEANCE (Super Edition)
OVERLOAD #8: OZARK PAYBACK
OVERLOAD #9: HUNTSVILLE HORROR

*coming soon:*
OVERLOAD #10: MICHIGAN MADNESS

OVERLOAD
Book
9

# HUNTSVILLE HORROR

## Bob Ham

BANTAM BOOKS
NEW YORK • TORONTO • LONDON • SYDNEY • AUCKLAND

Any similarity to persons, living or dead, places, businesses, governments, governmental entities, organizations, or situations, in existence or having existed, is purely coincidental.

HUNTSVILLE HORROR

*A Bantam Falcon Book / February 1991*

ISBN 0-553-28854-7

*Published simultaneously in the United States and Canada*

PRINTED IN THE UNITED STATES OF AMERICA

RAD          0 9 8 7 6 5 4 3 2 1

This one's for my friend Jerry Horn
—Southern Gentleman supreme—
scholar, retired jurist, avid reader,
and fellow amateur radio operator
who had the technological "pieces parts"
to bail me out when Murphy stepped in
and the circuits failed.

*Science should not concern itself in any way with the philosophical consequences of its discoveries.*

—LOUIS PASTEUR

*Let the vermin who abuse power, wealth, and knowledge show the scrowl of his ugly face. I will deal with him according to his deeds for the sake of the country I love and he should expect no mercy.*

—MARC LEE

# Chapter One

□ □ □

General A. J. Rogers III, commander of America's Delta Force, stood from behind the mahogany desk at the Pentagon in Washington, D.C. His round, pudgy face was flushed its normal red. When he spoke, his cheeks bounced in rhythm with his words. "Colonel Lee, Major Browne, I probably don't need to remind both of you that this mission is veiled in utmost secrecy. The president is scared shitless that some disgruntled bureaucrat is going to blow the lid off everything before the project is in place. That's why you're here. The president and I want to be damned sure nothing happens to this newfangled microreactor before it finds its way into orbit. If something goes astray, we'd all better plan to stow away on the next mission into outer space."

Colonel Marc Lee, Delta Force warrior turned Highway Warrior, managed a sheepish grin. "So we're dealing with a fire so hot that if anybody gets burned, we all burn? Is that the gist of it?"

"In a polite way, yes," General Rogers said.

"What are they gonna do with this thing once it's in space, General?" Major Carl Browne asked.

Rogers walked to the edge of his desk and sat down on the edge. "It's a microminiature nuclear reactor for

1

use on America's orbiting space station. That is, in the event the thing ever becomes a reality. Some environmental group has scooped word of its existence and they plan to do whatever they can to stop its use in space. The government and NASA are denying its very existence . . . claiming it is nonsense."

"All this fuss over something small enough to fit into a suitcase," Carl said. "Amazing."

"Don't let the size fool you, Major," Rogers said. "That little device is capable of supplying all of the electrical energy necessary to run an entire space station for ten years without refueling."

"What will they do with it in Huntsville, General?" Marc asked.

"Run it through the paces before the space shuttle takes it into orbit in a couple weeks. The launch date and time is classified. We don't know either exactly, but that's not the problem, men. This reactor can be modified to form the heart of a chain-reactive nuclear device. Simply translated, this little gem could form the core for a major nuclear weapon. Needless to say, there are a bunch of terrorist crackpots out there who would stop at nothing to get their hands on it. Hell of it is, if they accomplished that, the thing could be flown right out of the country in somebody's luggage and no one would be the wiser. That *cannot* and *will not* happen. Understood?"

"Perfectly," Marc replied. "One question, sir."

"Yes?"

"Isn't this a little out of our normal line of work?"

Rogers's cheeks jiggled with light laughter. "No, not at all. Sometimes the best way to fight crime is to prevent it. That's why you men will be transporting this device. There isn't a more secure or safer eighteen-wheeler in these United States than the Leeco rig.

There certainly is no one more qualified to handle the security for something like this than you and Carl. There is no better way. Period."

Carl walked to the heavy bright metal suitcase sitting on a table across the room. He looked at the microreactor device, pushed on the foam padding that held it, turned and faced General Rogers. "This thing looks like a stainless-steel garbage disposal. Look at the way it's shaped. This thing can run all the electricity needed for a space station for *ten* years?"

Rogers nodded. "That's what they tell me. Ten years. And that's even without the supplementary support of solar panels. Hard to believe, isn't it?"

"Damn sure is, General," Carl said.

"Who builds this thing, General?" Marc asked.

"It's the creation of a little-known outfit called STAR . . . Space Technology Advanced Research. They have a massive research, development, and testing facility built into the side of the Blue Ridge Mountains on the rural fringes of Roanoke, Virginia. Windy Gap Mountain, I think it's called. Hardly anyone outside of government or NASA circles knows they exist. I visited the facility once. You're right in the middle of it and you don't even know it's there. I found it spooky, to be perfectly honest. All that high-technology research right under the noses of the locals and hardly anyone knows what really goes on inside that mountain. Probably for the best, too. Some quack goes off and . . . well, you know how the scenario goes."

"All too well," Marc said.

"When do we leave?"

"Now."

"Sounds good," Carl said. "I have one question, General."

"Yes, Major."

"Who's knows we're transporting this device?"

Rogers smiled. "Good question. The president, me, and both of you. The scientists at Huntsville know only that someone will be making the delivery. They don't even know who or exactly when."

"So there shouldn't be any obstacles along the way?" Marc asked.

"You know the drill, Marc," Rogers said. "Never take anything for granted when you're dealing with this level of security. Anything is possible. Even the very best security clearances are not infallible. You both know that. But to answer your question, I don't anticipate any problems."

"Right," Marc said. The tone of his voice clearly indicated he wasn't convinced.

"One more thing," Rogers said. He walked to the metal suitcase and stared at the stainless-steel nuclear device meticulously packaged in the foam supports. "I want one of you with this device at all times. Don't let it out of your control until it is turned over to the people at NASA down at the Cape when the tests are finished in Huntsville. Eat with it, sleep with it, and I don't give a damn if you try to make love to it . . . just don't let this thing get away from you. Whatever the costs."

"Yes, sir," Carl said. "You say this deal should be finished and the shuttle ready to launch in the next ten days. Is that right?"

"Ten days. Two weeks. Somewhere around there," Rogers said.

Marc looked at Carl and saw worry in the big black warrior's face. He sought to reassure him. "We can handle it. Right, Carl?"

"Right," Carl said reluctantly, his face tense.

"Good, we have a few things to take care of and then we're off to Huntsville." Marc closed the lid on the suitcase and snapped the heavy-duty latches shut. He secured the Medeco padlocks and then the Sargent and Greenleaf combination locks on the front of the hinges. "All right, nice and secure. Combination memorized." He punched the digits on a digital keypad mounted on the outside of the case near the carrying handles, and a beep sounded. "Self-destruct detonator activated. Anybody messes with this little gem now without the proper key sequences and the combinations, and we'll all glow in the dark."

Carl's face hardened and every muscle in his body drew tight. "Wonderful. That sure makes me feel better."

J. Dermont Ashland enjoyed being in control. It didn't matter whether it was his children's future or the future of his self-made empire. Along with his abundant wealth came the special treatment he enjoyed so much, the feeling of superiority over everything he encountered, everything he touched. But even above his ability to control, Ashland enjoyed the secrecy that veiled his financial megabase . . . Louisville, Kentucky.

Some of Dermont's closest and most trusted associates, although they were indeed quite few in number, felt that the old tycoon carried the mystique too far. So far, in fact, that only few, if any at all, even knew that the *J* in his name stood for Jefferson. Dermont had dropped the "Jefferson" business during his childhood and insisted, when pressured, that his parents had merely used the initial *J* without further significance.

Ashland had come by his money the old-fashioned way—hard work and shrewd business practices. The shining stars in his financial zodiac were Ashland Chemical and ATS . . . Ashland Transport Service. The name of the latter reeked of simplicity, but first glances were very far from the truth. ATS wove a system of corporations and holding companies that controlled at least a score of medium-sized trucking concerns around the country into a complicated web. In the battle for financial dominance in Ashland's portfolio, ATS consistently perpetuated the old man's wealth by returning a healthy bottom line. He had come from the coal mines of eastern Kentucky to the top floor of his own high rise in downtown Louisville. ATS had made the trip much easier. The rise from a coal miner to an interstate common-carrier magnate, a trucking tycoon, had been made possible by Ashland's cunning and scores of eighteen-wheelers rolling freight across the pavement of the United States.

Ashland's personality and outward appearance were a lesson in deception. He looked more like a Baptist preacher than a ruthless businessman. His shiny white hair flowed back along the right side of his head in a wave that was seldom out of place. His sideburns were carefully cropped. And in his eyes danced the magnetism that swayed many a competitor to sign a deal before he made full and conscious evaluation of it. He was a fast talker, quick-tongued and shrewd, with a verbal delivery that almost made anyone he talked to look skyward for the impending onslaught of hellfire and damnation. But before the doom came, Dermont Ashland had secured that for which he had come. And such was the Ashland way . . . dazzle 'em and dominate 'em.

Ashland leaned forward in his chair and touched the intercom button that buzzed his secretary outside his office.

"Yes, Mr. Ashland?" the woman's voice said.

"Shirley, is my limousine ready?"

"One moment, Mr. Ashland, I'll check."

"Thank you." Ashland leaned back against the high-backed leather chair and spun around slowly. He clasped his hands together and rested his chin on them, his elbows on the arms of the chair. He looked out the window across the Louisville skyline. There he saw the interstate highway with trucks and cars moving like busy ants working in and out of a hill. A smile parted his lips. "Soon. Very soon."

The intercom buzzed on his desk and Shirley's voice came across the speaker. "Mr. Ashland, your driver is ready."

Ashland answered without turning around in his seat. He continued to focus on the skyline across the city. "Thank you, Shirley. I'll be out for the rest of the day. I'll call you when I get settled in."

"Yes, sir," Shirley replied. "Any special instructions before you leave?"

Ashland felt the smile on his lips widen. "Only one. If anyone calls for me, tell them I can't be reached until tomorrow at the earliest."

"Yes, sir. Have a good rest of the day, Mr. Ashland."

"Thank you, Shirley. That will be all."

Ashland studied the scenery for a long moment. Then he dropped his hands and stood from the high-backed chair. He walked to a private elevator ten feet from his desk. When he worked the digital combination, the door opened and he stepped inside for the ride to the underground parking garage beneath the Ashland Industries building. The door closed and the elevator started the smooth descent. When it stopped a minute later, the door opened into the private parking area. Ashland's chauffeur, dressed in a uniform of dark coat, hat, and pants, stood expectantly beside the rear door of the black Lincoln Town Car limo.

"Where to this afternoon, Mr. Ashland?" the driver asked cheerfully.

"Churchill Downs, Howard. I have a meeting there in one hour." Ashland replied.

"Yes, sir, Mr. Ashland," Howard said. He opened the rear door and waited for the old man to get comfortably seated. Satisfied that he was, Howard closed the door and got in the driver's seat. The limo was already running and Howard slipped it into gear. "Gonna watch the ponies again this evenin', sir?" Howard asked.

"Yes, for a while. A mixture of business and pleasure. I always enjoy the horses," Ashland said as he flipped through a report folder he had carried from the office.

"Beautiful day for the races," Howard said in an effort to strike up conversation. "Not a cloud in the sky. Ponies ought to run quick."

"Yes, they should."

Howard inched the limo forward from the exit of the parking garage onto the busy city street outside. He turned left and headed toward Broadway. Another left on Broadway and he saw the Third Street intersection in front of him. Howard made a left and headed south on Third. Several quiet minutes passed until Third intersected with Taylor Boulevard. Howard negotiated the right turn and drove along Taylor to the entrance of Churchill Downs. He drove beneath the giant sign that read WELCOME TO CHURCHILL DOWNS—HOME OF THE KENTUCKY DERBY.

"Gate seven, like always, sir?" Howard asked.

"Uh, no, Howard. Not this time. Take me to gate three," Ashland replied.

"Yes, sir. Gate three it is." Howard drove through the aisles of parked cars until he reached the entrance to gate three and on into the massive horse-racing facility. He stopped beside the curb and jumped from the driver's seat. In a flash, he was beside Ashland's door and swinging it open. "I'll park, sir. Shall I join you or wait with the car?"

Ashland scooted to the doorway and stepped out. "Tell you what, Howard. I plan to be a while." He reached into the breast pocket of his suit and removed his wallet. He counted off several bills and handed them to Howard. "Here's a thousand dollars. Go have yourself some fun with the ponies. Meet me back at the car in three hours. How's that?"

"Yes, sir," Howard said. His eyes lit up and he smiled as he accepted the money without question. "I'll be back here in exactly three hours. Thank you, sir."

"Very good," Ashland said. He smiled at Howard and walked toward the entrance to gate three.

Inside the sporting facility, Ashland made his way to the box seats and found the one he had reserved. He sat down, watched the ponies on the track, and waited.

Ten minutes passed and a man came into the box area. He moved through the aisles until he found a seat two seats away from Ashland. The man was sinister looking . . . dark-complected, dark hair, and very noticeable aftereffects of teenage acne. He looked straight ahead at the track when he spoke to Dermont Ashland. "Good afternoon, Mr. Ashland."

Ashland also kept his eyes on the track. He spoke to the man without ever acknowledging his presence with his eyes. "Good afternoon, Ramone. What do you have for me?"

"Good news," Ramone said. His voice was cool, callous. His eyes stayed fixed on the track. "They are moving the microreactor even as we speak. I have men on them. We will have it in our possession by this time tomorrow. We will be in control of every vital component of the facility within twenty-four hours."

"And then?" Ashland asked.

"And then we will be in the position to complete the project. Then we will be in control. Permanently."

"Good. Have a nice day," Ashland said.

"And you also, Mr. Ashland." Ramone stood and walked away. His eyes and Ashland's had not met through the entire conversation.

Two minutes passed and Ramone disappeared. Another man came from the opposite direction and stopped behind Ashland. "Yes, sir?"

"Frank, did you get all of that?"

"Every word," Frank said.

"Good. When we have control of the facility tomorrow, eliminate him. He knows too much."

"Yes, sir. It's done," Frank replied, and he left the way he came.

The trip along the beltway in Washington had gone smoothly enough—exactly the way Marc and Carl had planned it. They had waited to leave Washington near midnight, both preferring to drive at night instead of in the daylight. And if their timing was right, they would arrive in Huntsville sometime in early afternoon.

Traffic on I-66 westbound was the usual Washington madhouse until the Highway Warriors reached I-81 near Strasburg, Virginia. Marc drove the Leeco Freight Lines customized overroad rig and Carl rode shotgun on the passenger's side. I-81 had far less traffic than I-66 when Marc turned the rig south. Thinner traffic was welcome, but the trip along I-81 brought back memories of a time at the beginning of their war against the scourge that ravaged mankind. Both men knew that farther south, near Raphine and Steele's Tavern, if it were daylight, they could look to the east beyond White's Truckstop and see the mountain where Carl almost lost his life in the first of their many challenging wars. That was a long, long time ago, and time had healed the wounds. The experience, however, was etched in their minds forever.

"You know something, bro," Carl said. "I was just thinking. Can you imagine what some of the terrorists we've encountered in our lifetime could do with a little device like that thing back there in the suitcase?"

"That's something I'd rather not think about," Marc replied. "The world has enough kooks in it. Give some of them with enough money a chance at something like that microreactor and the world would be screwed. There'd be nowhere to hide. Damn frightening, isn't it?"

"Yeah, that's an understatement," Carl agreed. "How we gonna work it when we get to Huntsville? Switch shifts or both stay and alternate sleep scheds?"

"Doesn't really make any difference to me. You decide. I just know I'll rest much easier when that stainless-steel time bomb is on its way into outer space. Baby-sitting instant disaster isn't exactly my idea of a good time."

"Look on the positive side, bro," Carl said. "Twelve or thirteen hours from now that little gem will be safely inside the Marshall Space Flight Center in Huntsville."

"You say that like there's nothing to worry about," Marc said.

"Is there? You heard the general, nobody knows this thing is rolling. Right?"

Then the first shots ricocheted off the side of the rig. Marc glanced into the mirror and cut the rig hard right onto the shoulder. "Wrong!" he yelled as he fought to control the speeding Leeco Freight Lines overroad rig.

"What the hell is that?" Carl yelled.

"Shooter coming up fast on the left. An eighteen-wheeler. I see two in the cab. Gunner on the passenger's side." Marc manhandled the steering wheel and kept the rig from crashing into the guardrail. He swerved back to the left and returned to the highway. He immediately went into a zigzag pattern back and forth across the highway. The rig screamed from the stress of sudden turns and shifted weight. The 1400-horsepower diesel power plant gulped diesel fuel and belched out high-performance torque in the process. Marc watched the road ahead and glanced every couple of seconds into mirrors to keep track of the culprit.

"Shit!" Carl shouted. "Where'd he come from?"

"Beats me, but we gotta take him down before he causes one hell of a mess on the superslab. It may sound trite, but something tells me this is no chance encounter."

Marc steered hard, the Leeco rig groaning from the sudden strain. The other eighteen-wheeler crowded close along the left side of the high-tech Leeco rig. The gunner in the passenger's window leaned out and fired an automatic weapon, his image visible in the peripheral light from the rig's headlights. Hostile bullets whizzed through the air and slammed harmlessly into the Armor-shield body coating on Marc and Carl's rig. The technically advanced body armor could repel the small-arms fire as effectively as an army tank deflected BBs.

"We could outrun him," Carl shouted.

"Too risky. We mess up with forty tons of speeding overroad rig and we could kill a lot of innocent people. If we crash, the reactor might become unstable. I don't really know that much about the thing. It's not worth the risk."

"Then I guess we shoot it out, huh?"

"We gotta trash 'em and find out who they are. This wasn't supposed to happen. Somebody's messed up royally."

"I'd say," Carl agreed. "Baby, this ain't just a

leak . . . I'd say the dam's burst." He worked switches on the electronics console and activated the high-definition television cameras and the video tape recorders in the trailer of the Leeco rig. He flipped the computer screen to the armaments display and tilted it toward him. Out of habit, he moved the cursor to activate the Stinger miniguns, the 20mm cannons, and the retractable rocket pods built into the body of the rig. The screen displayed: ARMED. Carl reached under his seat and lifted his silenced Uzi submachine gun. "Cameras on. Collision Avoidance System activated. Weapons systems checked and armed. Electronic tracking engaged. ComSat-D link on active standby. I'm ready whenever you are, bro. Let the bastard take his best shot."

"I'll let him pass and then we'll trash him," Marc shouted.

"Deal," Carl replied.

Marc looked into the sparkling chrome rearview West Coast mirrors and watched the assaulting rig gain ground beside the Leeco machine. "Here he comes. Whoops, trouble."

"What kind?"

"Big time. The asshole leanin' out the window is holdin' a disposable rocket tube. This one's gonna get nasty. Hang on to your ass!"

# Chapter Two

□ □ □

Outward appearances are quite often deceptive.

Cass Miller knew that. He stared at the barren blacktop in front of the conventional Peterbilt diesel as he steered to the right of the double yellow line centered on the pavement. The overroad rig devoured the highway, leaving nothing but new ascending sequential digits on the odometer.

Miller took his eyes off the road occasionally to scan the Peterbilt's instrument console.

Everything appeared fine. Oil pressure was steady. Air pressure was stable. The battery voltage and amperage looked good, so that meant the alternator was still producing charging voltage despite the whine he had heard in the belts earlier when he found himself faced with a long, steep ascending grade. That was something he'd have to check after the delivery when he stopped for his next scheduled downtime at a truckstop. Odds were, something had slipped just a little and the belts would have to be tightened. That in itself wasn't a big deal. Downtime, on the other hand, was. Downtime meant no miles of lines and pavement in the rearview mirror, and that translated into no mileage money. But then, Interstate Commerce Commission rules *were* the rules of the game. Drive for a while and then park it . . . that's what the government rule book said.

Huntsville, Alabama, was like a ghost town at one o'clock in the morning. But that suited Miller just fine. No traffic meant no four-wheelers to get in the way and do stupid things on the superslab. The end result of the blessing was more miles and more money in less time.

Miller had driven for Ashland Industrial Chemical Company out of Kentucky for seven years. He had just turned thirty-five a week ago Sunday. And as the lines clicked by on the way to the security checkpoint, Cass Miller caught himself lost in thought about his life. Like the lives of so many people he knew, his hadn't turned out like he'd planned. The day after he had graduated from college, his on-again off-again fiancée had given him the joyous news that they were to soon become parents. Out of guilt and compassion, he married her three weeks later. Seven months after that, their daughter was born. A year, almost a year to the date, later, his wife decided she needed to "find herself."

Cass soon found himself divorced and the proud possessor of court-ordered alimony and child support that almost equaled three week's pay from his cushy office job for Allied Instruments.

That was in Illinois. It was also when Cass Miller decided it was time for a career change. He traded in his corporate stock for enough cash to pay for driving school out west. Eight weeks in the desert climate of Arizona didn't make him a fantastic driver, but it certainly opened the door for opportunities. It gave him a license to learn. And learn he did.

It took less than a year of riding with a partner at Ash-Chem to gain both a reputation of dependability and his own rig. Although Louisville wasn't *that* far from

Peoria, his ex-wife hadn't been able to find him and collect her monthly payments.

Miller had become an island. He had few acquaintances and even fewer friends. His life consisted of driving. For the first year after he left Peoria, he found himself plagued with a massive burden of self-imposed guilt for abandoning his daughter. But that all changed when the one person he had kept contact with in Peoria finally revealed that he had been living in a fool's paradise—along with that revelation came the indisputable evidence that the child wasn't really his. He learned that his ex-wife had later married a jock who graduated from college the same year he did. The jock had, in reality, fathered the child during an ongoing relationship that had continued even until two days before Miller had married the girl. When she confronted the guy with the facts, he decided he wasn't ready for the responsibility of parenthood. In reality, Cass had been her *second* choice, although he had also enjoyed the intimate pleasure of her company. The month she was suppose to have gotten pregnant, he hadn't touched her because he had been cramming for final exams. The jock, on the other hand, had willingly filled the void Cass had left vacant. None of that came to light until the Peoria friend exposed the facts better than three years after the fact.

None of that mattered now. By the time everything was out in the open, Cass had already changed his life and he loved it. Dan Post boots and denim jeans were more to his liking than dress suits and wingtips. He had decided that a life behind the wheel rolling eighteen wheels far surpassed the admiration of airheads in tight skirts passing by his desk on some godforsaken floor of a metropolitan office high rise.

All things considered, life still wasn't what he had thought it would be. Fact was, Cass liked it better this way. Much better. He had no one and no one had him. He was free and independent. And he thought that's the way a man should be.

The headlights cast a reflection off the caution markers at the security gate ahead. On each side of the security shack, there were hundreds of acres of pastureland complete with cattle. From the air and from the ground, the entrance to the massive installation appeared to be nothing more than active farmland.

From a hundred yards ahead, Miller could see the security guard holding his clipboard as he stepped into the night. Miller slowed the rig. He braked gently, tapping the brake pedal in slow and easy bursts to avoid the forward slosh of the liquid chemicals in the 2,400-gallon stainless-steel tank attached to the fifth wheel of the Peterbilt.

The rig came to a stop and Miller rolled down his window. He smiled at the guard, who appeared sleepy and unconcerned. "Good morning."

"Mornin' to you," the guard said. The words choked from his throat like he had been awakened from a deep sleep. He was middle-aged, probably in his fifties, and bored out of his mind. Graying hair met with the weathered skin at his forehead. A potbelly protruded from his midsection, the obvious product of too much beer and too many televised ballgames. "Need to see your security clearance and bill of lading."

"You'd think after all these years we'd be used to each other, Martin," Miller said with a grin as he leaned out the window. Martin Vance had been on the job as long as Miller had run the Huntsville delivery. Although their encounters had always been brief, they had become pleasantly routine.

"You know how government rules are, Cass. Somebody somewhere thinks maybe they could clone you or some such nonsense. How was the run?"

"No big deal. Miles of white lines and the hum of rubber grippin' the road," Miller said as he handed the bill of lading and his security clearance photocard for the Marshall Space Flight Center.

Vance took the paperwork and glanced at it nonchalantly. "I hear you boys been gettin' an unusual amount of snow up in Kentucky."

"Yeah. We've gotten to where we don't pay much attention to it anymore. Seems like almost every weekend we can count on gettin' three or four inches. It's a pain in the butt for drivin', but it's pretty just the same."

"I'm sure it is," Vance said. "Let me feed your card to the computer and I'll be back." Vance turned away and walked into the guard shack. He inserted the magnetic embossed card into the computerized card reader and waited for the clearance readout on the CRT display.

Four men materialized out of the darkness as if some stroke of black magic had set them on the ground where they stood. They were dressed in casual clothing with lightweight jackets and stocking caps, all dark. Their faces were hard, chiseled, mean. Each man was heavily armed with a small submachine gun and an automatic pistol in an exposed shoulder holster. Two of them leveled weapons on Martin Vance and the other two concentrated on Cass Miller in the cab of the Peterbilt.

One man appeared older than the others. He stepped toward the driver's door of the Peterbilt and pointed the automatic weapon at Miller's face. The assailant's face was cold and expressionless. When he spoke, his voice was firm, deep, and uncaring. "Out!" he said while his eyes bored through Miller with a penetrating hate-filled stare.

Miller swallowed hard and almost choked from the lump in his throat. His eyes widened. He felt himself trembling because he knew there was no escape. The armed men had the drop on him. Hands down. What he was seeing couldn't be possible . . . none of it. There was just no way this could happen . . . not in the United States of America.

Dr. Klaus von Wirth studied the printout from the sophisticated mainframe CAC Composition Analyst Computer system. He flipped through the green-bar pages slowly and methodically. His aging eyes stared through thick wire-rim bifocals as he digested the data. He stopped suddenly and rubbed his grizzled chin. The glasses slid to the tip of his nose and stayed precariously perched there for a long moment before he gently shoved them back into place.

Dr. von Wirth folded the printout open and laid it on the table in front of him. He pulled the glasses from his nose and put them on top of the data hardcopy. For a moment, he stared around the brightly lit laboratory through eyes that saw, but didn't fully comprehend what they focused upon. Those eyes were, without question, failing him now. They had been for years, but now the failure seemed to manifest itself more with each passing day. He leaned back in the soft high-backed chair and rubbed his eyes vigorously as if he were trying to stimulate them with the second joint of each index finger. Dr. von Wirth knew that would do them no good, but it eased their tiredness. Made them feel better, and even that much relief was welcome.

When Dr. von Wirth removed his fingers, the room seemed to fill with swirling white lights of the kind frequently seen by a person who has just sustained a moderate blow to the head. Seeing stars, he thought it was called. He squinted hard against the bright white fluorescent lights and stared at an array of chemical-analysis paraphernalia arranged on the white Formica counter ten feet across the room. How long had it been since he'd come to this place? How long had he dwelled in this antiseptic, almost sterile world beneath the real world? *Twenty years?* No, more like thirty. Or was that actually *forty? Could it really be forty years?*

He had to stop and think about it. He had been thirty-four when the men in beige trench coats and Stetson hats with their brims flipped down in front had whisked him from Germany in the middle of the night. They had promised him freedom and a laboratory furnished with anything and everything he needed now, or for that matter, ever would need for as long as he lived. They promised him protection, political asylum, and complete anonymity. The president of the United States had even greeted him before he ended his journey at this place. And he would never forget that day. The day President Truman shook his hand and greeted him with a warm, friendly smile. No, he could never forget it.

He was seventy-four now. And what was the trite American cliché? *Time flies when you're having fun?* Yes, that was it. He wasn't sure about the fun, but time had flown, taking in its wake the threads of his life and the bounty of his work.

Through it all, the first promises of the Americans had been kept. Never once had *they*, those unseen people who form the government, broken a promise or gone back on their word. Dr. von Wirth had everything he needed to effectively go about his work for the good of mankind. And, in exchange, he had worked effectively all those years.

His laboratory occupied slightly over 43,000 square feet, almost an acre. The entire environment was controlled with absolute precision. Outside air was pumped into an ultra-high-efficiency biological filtration system from concealed air vents on the ground five hundred feet from the ceiling of the lab. Twin wells from the water table above the underground facility supplied ample water for research and human consumption. It, too, was filtered and treated by active water-filtration devices. Heat was gathered by water heat pumps whose coils were submerged in the natural underground water channels. Humidity control, necessary for human comfort as well as for the stability of various experiments, was maintained by a bank of humidifiers and dehumidifiers linked to a central humidistat detection system that constantly monitored each room of the facility. Humidity could be maintained to within one-tenth of one percent by proper programming of the control microprocessor.

Electrical energy for von Wirth's research lab was supplied by two redundant miniature nuclear reactors capable of emitting a constant one-megawatt of combined output for an indefinite period of time. One large and secure room contained the reactors and the regulation system for the entire complex. Only von Wirth and three of his technicians had authorized access to the energy room.

The ground atop the facility resembled farmland. Cattle, in fact, grazed on lush grass during the day. At night, a weathered wooden barn provided shelter for the animals, should foul weather hover over Huntsville. But the pasture was a mask of deception and the barn provided shelter for more than the beasts that dined on the bounty of the soil. A small room in the northeast corner divided from the rest of barn by rough-hewn oak lumber completed the superficial guise. There, beneath a thick layer of hay strewn randomly upon the floor, lay the hidden entrance to the first tunnel beneath the ground that led to an elevator shaft to the east a hundred feet away. That shaft, twenty-five feet square and five hundred feet deep, was the only entry and exit into the facility—or at least the only one most people knew about. To reach the elevator, every person passed through three levels of security. Each level, or lock, was pressurized and accessible only with an authorized magnetic card etched with a Level 1-A security encode. Should a bogus card somehow find its way into any of the three locks, the cardholder was immediately entrapped within the lock until security personnel could take the defensive action deemed necessary. And although that action had never been required, the minds of those with authorization harbored little doubt as to the end result of security intervention. In all likelihood, the intruder would suddenly and mysteriously vanish from the face of the planet.

All who knew of the underground research facility knew such extreme measures were a requirement if the security of the clandestine research were to remain intact. After all, chemical and biological warfare had been outlawed, banned by mutual accord of the world's prominent leaders at the Geneva conventions. Even the great mastermind Albert Einstein once said that he didn't know what weapons would be used to fight World War III, but if those weapons were nuclear, World War IV, would be fought with rocks and clubs. But then Albert Einstein hadn't known about the research beneath the ground at Huntsville's Redstone Arsenal. If he had, he would have known that if the weapons developed in the underground labs were ever used, there would likely be no one left to fight the next big war. Why? Because there was no defense from lethal self-generating viruses and deadly chemical compounds that, once breathed, caused the red and white blood cells within the human body to separate, resulting in almost instant agonizing death.

Einstein, like the rest of the world, hadn't known that. But the terrorists who wanted control of the facility did. And soon, so would everyone else, if the scheduled shuttle launch went okay.

Cass Miller thought he was looking into a mirror. Problem was, the mirror image of himself he saw squatting on the pavement between the rig and the security shack held a submachine gun . . . pointed straight at his face.

Miller realized his voice was trembling, but he was finally able to choke the words from his throat. "What do you guys want? Man, I'm not haulin' anything worth all this firepower."

The hard-faced man with the subgun jerked the muzzle in a harsh gesture that Miller took to mean "get out."

"Okay, okay. I'm movin'. Be careful with that thing. I wouldn't want it to go off." Miller moved his left hand to the door handle and gently pulled the lever. The door opened and he stepped to the footstep below the threshold. He swung around and grabbed the handrail as he climbed nervously from the cab. His shaky feet touched the pavement and that's when he realized how rubbery his legs were. He also realized he was damn scared. His stomach churned, bitter acid, generated by fear, burning his insides. And to judge by the faces of the hardcases holding the heavy firepower, there was ample reason to be afraid.

The lead man with the chiseled face raised his right hand and snapped his black-gloved fingers. Another man appeared from the darkness. This one wore a uniform exactly like the one Martin wore and the man was the spitting image of old Martin.

Miller's eyes widened. He couldn't believe what he saw; a new reality had appeared from the darkness and was now in total control. Miller breathed a deep sigh as another shattering tremor of unadulterated fear quaked through him. "Jeez, what's happening?" he mumbled beneath his breath. But the hunch forming deep inside his flaming gut told him he really didn't want to know. Not now. Not never.

The gunman inside the guard shack with Martin nudged the muzzle of his subgun against the old guard's side and pushed him outside. Martin's eyes were saucer-wide and filled with fear.

"What are you gonna do to us?" Martin asked. His voice quavered as the words left his trembling lips. And even before he asked the question, he was sure he, like Miller, didn't want to know the answer.

The man with the subgun nudged the muzzle further into Martin's ribs. The old guy jerked upright from the jabbing pain. He moved a couple of steps and thought about the old Model 10 Smith & Wesson .38 Special in the worn leather holster on his hip. There was no doubt about it, the revolver was no match for the hardcases toting Uzis. Martin considered making a try at unsheathing the old .38, but better judgment told him to play it cool. Something wasn't right here and he knew it. Why had the cold-steel faces holding the subguns even allowed him to keep the revolver? The question plagued him while the answer evaded him. Then it hit him. Maybe they wanted him to make a move for the gun, needed a reason to perforate him with hot 9mm death. A reason to punch his time clock for good. With that thought in mind, Martin decided he wouldn't give them what they wanted. No way.

No one moved. The man nearest Miller kept his eyes locked with Miller's. The bore of the man's subgun stayed firmly aimed at Miller's midsection, ready to drill through the flesh and bone with the touch of his finger on the curved steel trigger.

Miller's breath was coming hard. He felt like he was suffocating, his lungs tight and singeing with each deliberate motion of his chest. He inspected the faces of the hardcases and then he looked at Martin. He saw helplessness radiating from the old guard's eyes. And at that moment, Miller knew he had to do something . . . anything. Anything other than stand there like a patsy and let the machine-gun-toting animals shoot them both like rats in a sewer.

The main hardcase raised his left hand again. The other men raised their heads in full attention. He looked at Miller, his eyes boring through him. "Across the road. Now! Move!"

"What?" Miller asked, pretending he didn't understand.

"Now," the man said again. "Move to the edge of the field."

"Look, guy," Miller said. "If it's the rig you want, take it. Take the load, too, if you want. It isn't mine anyway. I just drive the thing. Let me and old Martin go. We'll go have a few drinks and forget any of this crap ever happened. How 'bout it?"

"I'm sorry, I can't do that," the main hardcase said. Ice laced his voice and fire radiated from his eyes. "That isn't according to plan."

# Chapter Three

□ □ □

Carl was already taking defensive action. He moved the electronic sight for the side-mounted machine guns. When the circular sight found the side of the renegade rig, Carl fingered the firing mechanism. A shudder reverberated over the Leeco rig as twin .30-caliber machine guns unleased a hellstorm volley of 7.62mm sizzlers. The heavy 180-grain copper-jacketed projectiles chewed through aluminum and upholstery as they ate their way through the pursuers' cab.

It worked.

The men in the assaulting rig weren't prepared for such defensive firepower. The lethal hellstorm took them by total surprise. The gunner lost his grip on the rocket tube at almost the instant he triggered the firing mechanism. A streak of white expanding gases marked the vapor trail as the LAW-class rocket streaked past both rigs and slammed into the pavement on an incline far in front of them. The ground beneath both speeding rigs trembled from the impact as debris and fire rained from the sky up ahead.

"Hit 'em again!" Marc yelled.

Carl touched off another burst and the Leeco rig emitted its resonant rumble when the twin guns pelted hot death into the leading edge of the big hostile rig.

"Damn Peterbilts are tough as nails," Carl mumbled disgustedly.

"Okay, let him pass."

"Got it," Carl replied.

The renegade rig kept up the assault. The shooter was back now, the smaller automatic weapon in his hands again. Both rigs swerved across the roadway like snakes on hot coals.

Marc glanced out his window and saw the silhouette of the shooter when the guy raised the autogun to fire. "Here it comes."

A stream of flying death pellets slammed into the bullet-resistant glass at Marc's head. The sophisticated transparent material survived the onslaught unscathed. The shooter's death slugs spent their energy harmlessly and slammed into the pavement below.

"Nice try, dickhead," Carl cried. "Eat this." He trained the electronic sight on the front cowling of the big Peterbilt Class 8. Then he touched off a three-round burst from the rotating 20mm cannons retracted inconspicuously into the front cowling of the Leeco rig.

Once more, the Leeco machine trembled from the recoil as deafening roars of unrelenting death sailed toward their objective. The barrage slammed into the Peterbilt and caused the front end to sail skyward into a thousand fiery fragments. The big rig listed out of control, fear etched across the faces of the men riding in the cab.

"Almost," Marc said.

Then the driver of the renegade machine cut hard right in a last-ditch effort to run the unyielding Leeco eighteen-wheeler off the highway.

Marc cut right also, his steering guided by the electronic Collision Avoidance System that Carl had activated at the onset of trouble. He stomped the accelerator and the giant rig shot forward with a new burst of life from the customized diesel power plant beneath the gleaming red cowling that penetrated the air in front of the men of Overload.

Carl snapped off another burst from the machine guns. A roar of repetitious thunder livened the air again. This time, the deadly hornets chewed rubber and pavement at the rear of the renegade trailer.

The driver of the bandit rig was unyielding now also. He cut back toward the Leeco machine. The CAS in the Leeco cab automatically avoided a collision.

Another burst of heavy firepower fingered by Carl and the right rear tires on the bandit machine burst apart. They flapped around the rims and disintegrated into bits of flying black rubber, sailing into the air, pushed backward by the rig's slipstream.

The big forty-eight-foot trailer swerved on the bandit rig, seeking its own course of travel. The driver fought for control as the big rig shot from one side of I-81 to the other and then back again.

Marc glanced at the speedometer . . . ninety-two miles per hour. Ahead, traffic was starting to get congested. Both rigs rolled toward the top of the incline where the unguided rocket had plowed pavement from the crust of the earth. "Here comes the pothole."

Both rigs cut at almost the same time. The bandit went left and Marc swerved right to miss the five-foot crater left from the impact of the hostile rocket.

Both missed it.

They came back together. The shooter reappeared, his head and hands visible around the leading edge of the renegade trailer. And in his hands, the little autogun belched a blazing stream of death missiles intended for the Highway Warriors.

His efforts were futile. Just as before, the bullets

slammed into the state-of-the-art ballistic glass on the Leeco rig and uselessly spent their deadly foot-pounds of potentially fatal energy.

Both rigs crested the hill. The bandit rig held the lead by a cab length. Marc wanted to keep it that way.

"Oh, baby!" Carl shouted when he saw the highway ahead.

Marc tapped the accelerator and closed the gap until the front of the Leeco rig almost touched the tail of the renegade trailer. He looked ahead and saw a dozen or more cars on the highway in front of them, their headlights illuminating the valley below. The roadway dropped off sharply on a descent for a mile and a half or more. At the bottom of the decline, the road shot back up in a long incline toward the top of another long, steep grade. But at the bottom, a long bridge spanned a gorge that appeared, with the aid of the headlights from the cars ahead, to be a river bottom. And then Marc made a decision.

The bandit rig swerved across the highway. He was closing fast on several cars. The drivers saw him and spun out to the side of the highway. Both rigs shot past fear-filled faces and horrified looks, glaring back in the beam of headlights.

Marc steered hard to avoid a car that had braked abruptly in the middle of the highway. The Leeco rig rocked from the sudden turn, but Marc quickly regained full control. "Take him down when we bottom out. Don't let them start up the other side."

"Done," Carl replied. He scanned the renegade rig into the electronic sight and readied the firepower. He rested his finger on the firing mechanism and started a mental countdown.

The renegade smashed into the side of a station wagon and knocked it from the pavement into the embankment beside the highway. Headlights sent spiraling beams of light through the night. The hostile driver fishtailed hard to the right and then back to the left before he finally regained control of eighteen-wheels of speeding death.

The tables had turned now; the hunter had unwittingly become the hunted. Marc closed until he was beside the renegade. The rear end of the bandit trailer rested against the pavement on what remained of the wheel rims. Sparks flew with every foot of pavement the steel rim chewed and sliced.

Three seconds.

The bottom was near now. The bandit fought for survival as cars swerved to avoid impact. The bridge ahead closed fast as white lines became more of a streak flashing by in a deathly mirage.

"Now!" Carl yelled. He twitched the firing button and dealt the shooters a death hand . . . two pair, two deadly rockets from each side of the Leeco rig. The retractable pods were locked in place for firing, and four swirling streams of fiery contrail and smoke streaked through the air, found metal, and devoured it like angry piranhas.

A massive explosion sent an intensely glowing orange fireball and a hellstorm of debris spiraling into the air. The darkness came alive with the flash of fire and death. Marc had backed off the accelerator and permitted the Leeco rig to coast at an even hundred miles per hour.

The renegade rig tumbled into its final death throes and riveted from the highway, tearing a two-hundred-foot section of guardrail with it. The rig bounced into the air and seemed suspended in a blazing halo of fire that lit the river valley for a microsecond. Then it settled back to the ground and plummeted from sight over the lethal lip of the gorge. The fall was more than 425 feet. When the bandits and their chariot smashed into the ground below, all that remained were bits and pieces of evil suddenly digested by the unrelenting force of cleansing hellfire.

Cass Miller was scared to death. Hijacking was one thing, but a giant stainless-steel tank of some newfangled chemical concentrate was hardly worth getting killed over. And at this moment, the likelihood was that death would be his new keeper. He tried to make his voice believable and not reveal the sickness churning inside his stomach. "All I understand is that you guys came from the darkness like the devil himself put you here. You got the guns, boys. You're the boss. Anything you want."

"Move. Now," the hardcase said. He motioned with the barrel of the subgun once more. The universal language spoken from the business end of an automatic weapon was very clear.

Miller understood that universal language all too well. He moved forward a step or two and shot a fast glance toward Martin. "Looks like they got us, Martin."

The old guard nodded in agreement. His eyes were still saucer-wide and his face was pale, deathlike. He stood rigid, every muscle in his body tense with fear. His breathing was deliberate and shallow, each lungful a conscious struggle.

"No chatter," the main hardcase said. "Just walk very slowly to the other side of the road."

"Right," Miller said obediently. He took another step and lunged to his right, his right arm out, stiff-arming Martin with all the force he could transmit to the end of his hand.

The old guard was stunned. He fell back, his

balance gone. When he tripped, he slammed into the man with the subgun nearest him. Both men crashed into the wall of the guard shack and then plummeted to the pavement.

Miller made a frantic death-defying dive. He jerked the automatic weapon from the downed shooter's hands and twisted the muzzle around while his finger found the trigger. A short burst of deathfire and scorching lead belched from the subgun's rifled bore. Miller moved fast and zippered the guy from his balls to this tonsils with another deadly burst.

"Take him!" the main hardcase yelled hysterically. He sought a target with the barrel of his Uzi, but couldn't fine one. He dropped low to one knee and waved the autogun's muzzle in total desperation.

The other shooters moved to get rounds off at Miller. The men scrambled and sought cover, but there was none.

Miller spun to the left on the pavement and fired another staccato from the Uzi. Hot pelting lead chewed away flesh; blood-splattered bone fragments sprayed into the night shrouded by a sea of crimson red mist. A second hardcase dropped to the pavement in screaming agony. His screams fell silent when a twitch of Miller's trigger sent a three-round burst into his face. Three circular holes appeared where his nose had been, but quickly vanished in a red river of spurting blood.

The man who looked just like Cass Miller opened fire with his autogun. He peppered the guard shack with 9mm deathfire, but the hellstorm was wasted into inanimate wood.

Miller rolled two turns, came up, and jumped to his knees to fire. That's when he heard the bark of Martin's .38 Special behind him. The old guard had the narrow-barreled Smith & Wesson spitting hot sizzling death.

The .38 slugs tagged a hardcase in the shoulder, slowing him. The man hesitated for a microinstant and Miller pumped the remainder of the autogun's magazine into him from point-blank range. The mortally wounded shooter stood suspended for a few seconds, vibrating like a flag in a windstorm.

The main steel-faced hardcase fired a burst of hellfire toward Miller.

Miller fell prone and rolled. He stopped beside the second fallen death menace and grabbed the dead man's subgun. He dropped the first Uzi and squeezed the trigger of the one he had just liberated.

A volley of 9mm death pellets sizzled through the night. The pellets tore through flesh and shattered bone. Long spurts of blood splayed on the air. The sailing droplets covered Miller, dotting him bright red with spatter. And then he felt Martin fall dead at his feet. He realized his own copper-jacketed hornets had missed their mark and the main hardcase had chewed Martin to dead hamburger with a burst of subgun hellfire.

The main hardcase ducked right.

Miller kicked Martin's dead body out of the way and rolled left, seeking balance and a target. And then the searing death pellets tore through him like white-hot rods of steel. He felt them, many of them, and they came all at once. The pain stopped in a heartbeat, but the impact felt like what Miller had always imagined the front bumper of a speeding Peterbilt would feel like if it found flesh on the open road. He felt the subgun slip from his dying hands and then the euphoria of tranquil darkness overwhelmed him. At first, it felt like an orgasm that would never end. It was chilling, nerve tingling, and relaxing all at the same time. Then it ended as quickly as it started, and Cass Miller knew he was dead. But somehow, neither his body nor his mind seemed to care because the moment of horror that preceded the soothing tranquillity was over. The darkness had taken that away.

The main hardcase jumped to his feet, the muzzle of his weapon trained on Miller's perforated motionless body. He grabbed a small handheld two-way radio from a sheath at the small of his back. He pressed the talk switch and spoke into the speaker microphone on the front grille of the little unit. "Insurgence Unit-one, this is IU-two. This position is compromised with casualties. Control assumed. Let 'em roll."

The Ashland Chemical eighteen-wheel tanker negotiated its way through the turns inside the Marshall Space Flight Center compound. Ahmad Nadimi drove. The fact that he had never seen the inside of the facility made no difference. And even the fact that he had never been on American soil until twenty-four hours ago didn't prove to be an insurmountable obstacle. He weaved through the maze of streets and buildings like a veteran. He had committed the satellite-imagery photographs of the entire compound to his flawless memory in much the same way he had perfectly assumed the identity of Cass Miller. Months had been spent learning everything there was to know about Miller and his life. He had even practiced the man's Midwestern accent until he could duplicate it flawlessly and effortlessly. It was, after all, a strategic part of the plan.

Nadimi reached the eastern back quadrant of the compound, several miles from the front security gate. He rolled the rig to a stop near an old barn sitting in the middle of the field. He flipped the switch on the windshield-mounted spotlight and twisted the handle until the bright beam of white light fell upon the ground beside the barn. Then he saw them. The concealed fill pipes to the underground chemical-storage containers.

He switched the light off and waited. Seconds passed and then more headlights appeared from the darkness beside the last row of buildings before the rocket-engine testing pads.

IU-two.

Three more overroad rigs laden with a very special cargo: insurgents.

Nadimi sat patiently and watched until all three rigs drove beside him and stopped. The driver of the rig nearest him opened the door and climbed from the cab.

Nadimi did likewise.

The men met between the rigs and exchanged brief greetings.

"Nadimi, I see there have been no unconquerable problems," the man said.

"No, Jon, nothing we weren't able to contain. And I am no longer known to you as Ahmad Nadimi. You must remember my name is Cass Miller for the duration of our mission," Nadimi said.

"I was told there were casualties. What became of the bodies?" Jon asked.

"Neatly disposed of. We lost two men in the attack. We terminated two foolishly brave ones at the guard shack. All of the bodies were stripped of any metal that might be a problem and we put them in the chemicals up there in the tank," Nadimi said. He smiled and gestured to the huge stainless-steel chemical tank behind his newly acquired Peterbilt cab. "Call it emergency improvising. They should be reduced to untraceable liquid in a few more minutes. The chemicals in this truck's tank are very concentrated and very, very powerful. The slosh in the tank on my short trip in here should have aided substantially in the decomposition of the remains. Their presence will no longer pose a problem."

"Ah, then our people died well?"

"Bravely, and with dignity. That I assure you," Nadimi said.

"No more can a man ask," Jon said. "We must complete this segment of our mission. Daylight will come to us soon. Are we ready?"

"Ready," Nadimi replied.

Jon raised his right hand and more men appeared from the cabs of the overroad rigs. They gathered around him. "You, as team leaders, have been well briefed. Get your people and we will move out."

The men scattered in pairs. Each pair ran to the locked doors of the trailers behind the overroad rigs. They opened the locks, swung the doors open, and twenty armed insurgents descended from the trailers of each rig. The men quickly formed into three teams and met at the front of the rigs.

"Brothers," Jon said. "You know your missions. Go about them with determined dedication."

Two groups of the men turned without hesitation and disappeared into the night. Two more units of two men each ran toward two of the overroad rigs. The sound of diesel engines firing filled the night around the old barn. Both rigs went into gear at the same time and pulled away. They headed to opposite sides of the Marshall Space Flight Center compound to fulfill their treacherous mission.

Nadimi and Jon stood side by side facing the remaining group of armed insurgents. Jon looked at his watch, then at Nadimi. "Are you ready?" he asked. "It is time."

"I'm ready," Nadimi said, smiling. "On to our moment of shining greatness."

Jon took the lead. He ran toward the barn, Nadimi beside him. When they reached the inside of the frail wooden building, Nadimi reached into a fanny pack and removed a can of black spraypaint. He climbed the wooden slats of a barn stall and painted the concealed lens of a closed-circuit television camera. When he was finished, he jumped down and lifted the top of a hay-covered trapdoor and climbed down the ladder that led to a platform ten feet below.

Jon and the insurgents followed one at a time. When they were all gathered on the platform, Nadimi lifted a magnetically encoded plastic card from his shirt pocket and slipped it into the security system's card reader. Shortly thereafter, a beeper sounded and the clay dirt wall slid open and away to his right. He entered and inserted the card in another electronic card reader.

A voice crackled over a wall-mounted speaker. "Yes, Mr. Miller. Please state the nature of your request."

Nadimi, posing as Cass Miller, answered, "Another chemical delivery for you. It's time to check the integrity of the valves and tank on your end. You know the drill, guys."

"Ah," the voice said. "Time must fly. I didn't realize it had been three months already. Has it?"

"Three months and two days to be exact."

"All right," the voice said from within Dr. von Wirth's underground laboratory. "I'll open the next lock for you and you must work your card from there on. And, as you say, you know the drill."

"Could do it in my sleep. Matter of fact, I've dreamed about it a few times. I keep thinkin' I'm gonna get trapped in that mole hole you got down there."

"Please, Mr. Miller. Just enter. Careful with your comments about our delightful domicile beneath the earth. To you it's a mole hole. To us it's home. See you in a few minutes."

"The things I do to make a living," Nadimi said, playing the role for all he was worth. "Catch you in five."

Nadimi inserted the card into the reader and waited for the security lock to open. He looked back at Jon and the armed insurgents and nodded when the door to his left, which looked more like a wall, opened abruptly.

They made their way through the security locks until they reached the elevator shaft. When the proper encode was entered into the electronic lock on the elevator, the door opened.

"Quietly," Nadimi warned in a soft whisper. "Not a sound." He pointed to a small microphone and speaker in one corner of the elevator. "They listen down below."

When all twenty-two men were on the elevator, Nadimi entered the sequence to close the door and start the descent to the laboratory five hundred feet below them.

The descent took two minutes. The elevator coach slipped to a slow stop and the door opened. The armed insurgents rushed from the open door and aimed their assault rifles at everything and everyone in sight.

"No alarms. Not a word," Jon said coldly from behind an Uzi submachine gun perched on his hip.

"What is this madness?" a white-coated lab technician asked through trembling lips.

Jon smiled, his face hard and mean. "This is the horror you have always dreamed about in your darkest moments. This is the revelation to all the world of your senseless stupidity. This is *your* Armageddon."

# Chapter Four

□ □ □

Carl deactivated the Leeco rig's weapons systems while Marc put miles between them and the fiery remains of the bandit rig. They had watched behind them in the mirrors and on the closed-circuit HDTV monitor. The gorge below the I-81 bridge glowed red and orange from the wasted burning shell of the renegade rig.

Carl finished the disarming procedure and then looked over at Marc. He could see the worried look on his partner's face in the ambient glow of the headlights reflecting off the highway ahead. "Well, I guess you're gonna tell me that we just happened to be in the wrong place at the right time, huh? I mean none of that firepower was *really* intended for you and me, was it?"

"I didn't say that," Marc replied. A serious smile split his hard face.

"Yeah, I know you didn't say it, but you were sure thinkin' it. That's why I said it for you."

"I was trying to rationalize it all out, that's all," Marc said.

"Right. You know damned good and well, you're thinkin' exactly what I'm thinkin', aren't you?"

Marc steered, his eyes locked to the road. He

**41**

occasionally checked the rearview mirrors to be sure the lone bandit had really been alone. "You mean how anyone would know where the microreactor was and when it was being moved?"

"We been together too long. You know that? Maybe we should just start numbering the thoughts and call out a number when we're thinkin' something instead of wasting so damned much time talkin'."

"Might work," Marc said. "You're worried, aren't you?"

"Now what on earth do I have to be worried about? Should I be worried just because some wiseass tried to blow the rig off the highway? Should it concern me that I'm hauling some sophisticated piece of stainless steel that the United States government says doesn't even exist? What do I have to be worried about?"

"Yep, I knew it. You're worried. Well, if it's any consolation to you, so am I. I think our main concern right now should be getting that hunk of hightech stainless steel to Huntsville. Once we get it there and delivered to the proper people, we can work out the security details. Something obviously has slipped through the hallowed portals of security in Washington. We got a shitter in the nest somewhere. Question is, who, and how high up?"

Carl leaned back in the airshock seat and stretched his legs up on the dashboard. He stared through the windshield and watched the white lines speed past the high-tech Leeco machine in a synchronized blur. "Yeah, that hit back there is buggin' the piss outta me. If they wanted the device and they knew we were carryin' it, why did they take the chance on trashin' the rig and having the thing damaged or destroyed? Something ain't right, bro."

"Maybe you nailed it," Marc replied.

"How's that?"

"Maybe they really didn't want the reactor. Maybe they didn't want anyone else to have it either and decided to trash it."

Carl rubbed his chin and contemplated the possibility. "That's a thought. And if you're right, it didn't matter whether they offed us or not. If they trashed the nuke, then they got what they wanted."

"Bingo!" Marc said.

"But on the other hand," Carl said, "they could have just wanted to take the rig down, terminate us, and steal the device. Maybe they weren't expecting the retaliation to be so intense."

"One thing about it," Marc said. "Those assholes will never be able to answer the question."

"Breaks my heart," Carl said.

"Yeah, a lotta sadness in the world, huh?"

Carl jerked his feet from the dashboard and sat upright. He reached for the Uzi at the edge of the seat on the floorboard. He was startled, his face suddenly chiseled rock hard. "You hear that?"

Marc looked at Carl. "What? What's wrong?"

"Chopper. You didn't hear the chopper?"

"No, I didn't. Are you sure?"

"Maybe I'm hearing things. I could have sworn I heard a chopper make a low pass somewhere behind us."

The swoosh of swirling blades churned the air above the Leeco rig. The unmistakable roar of the chopper's engine drowned out the purring sounds of the giant diesel engine beneath the hood of the Leeco rig.

"I heard it that time," Marc said excitedly. "I don't like the sound of it either."

Carl quickly laid the Uzi on his lap and focused his attention on the computer screen mounted between the seats on the instrument console. He moved switches, set systems, armed all of the Leeco rig's defensive and offensive weapons systems. "Something's really out of line here, bro. We been set up. Tell me that chopper just happened to make a low pass over *our* rig?"

"Which way did he go?" Marc asked. He tried to look through the upper edge of the windshield and steer the rig at the same time.

"He went to our left, to the east. Sounded like he banked north," Carl said.

"If he's a bandit, he's probably coming in from the rear for a strafing pass."

Carl watched the computer screen. Then he shifted his attention to the HDTV monitor. He panned the cameras around the sky above the highway, searching for the marker lights on the chopper. "If he's not a bandit, he's nuts. Sucker couldn't have been more than a hundred feet over us when he passed."

"Yeah," Marc said. "Takes a damn good pilot to fly like that in these hills in the dark."

"Right," Carl said. "A damn good pilot or an idiot. I don't see him on the monitor."

"He's out there," Marc replied. "Could be we're just a little too jumpy. What do you think?"

"We *are* jumpy. Got a right to be. Too much shit happenin' here to suit me. This mission was supposed to be such a big secret, now everything's gone haywire. I don't like it. I don't like it at all."

The night sky in front of the Leeco rig burst alive with a roaring orange fireball. The blazing object struck the pavement fifty yards in front of the rig.

All hell broke loose.

Fire was everywhere. Shooting, hungry tongues of flames licked toward the dark sky in unforgiving ferocity. The highway became a fierce inferno waiting to digest anything and everything within its flaming reach. Beyond the towering flames, the helicopter hovered above the highway like the lethal silhouette of some mechanized monster. And then the night became light with an ultrabright portable sun mounted on the undercarriage of the chopper.

"Shit!" Carl yelled. "Big-time trouble."

Marc slammed the brakes on the Leeco rig and tried to slow it before it entered the flaming gauntlet. He looked right, then left, for a place to go. A way to avoid flaming death. But the chopper pilot had chosen his strike point well. The fire raged in the middle of a high-cut slope. The embankments rose awkwardly on both sides of the road. There was absolutely nowhere to go except into the jaws of the lethal fire. When he realized the rig couldn't stop in time, he let off the brakes, grabbed another gear, and floored the accelerator. "Here we go," he screamed.

"Don't forget the ballast fuel tanks under the trailer," Carl yelled. He aligned the electronic sights for the LAR rockets on the nose of the chopper at the same time.

"Too late to worry about that now," Marc shouted. He steered the rig for the center of the fire and held the pedal all the way to the floor. His muscles ached from the sudden tension and he felt beads of perspiration building on his brow. He gritted his teeth and held the wheel tightly. "This may be it, bro. It's been real."

"Oh no!" Carl yelled as his finger tightened on the switch for the firing mechanism. "It ain't over yet. These bastards have pissed me off!"

"Too late," Marc screamed when he saw the fiery trail from the air-to-surface missile leave the pod on the side of the hovering helicopter.

Jon moved in the direction of the lab technician. He held his Uzi in a tightly clenched fist and shoved it into the technician's face as he spoke through gritted teeth. "Up and away from the security-system activator."

The technician's face was as ghostly white as the lab jacket he wore. He stared at the Uzi-toting intruder through terrified, disbelieving eyes. He hesitated, unable to move or speak.

Jon leaped over the small slick-topped counter and grabbed the technician by the collar of his lab jacket. He jerked him from his seat and slammed him to the top of the counter on his back. He moved the muzzle of the Uzi to the tech's lips and shoved it inside his mouth. "Hear me well. I am now in control here. You do what I say, when I say it. If it looks like I have to tell you anything more than once, I'll just shoot you and be finished with it. I am a man of little patience and even less compassion. Do I establish my point clearly?"

The technician couldn't speak. Blood trickled from his open mouth and spilled onto the counter top. He managed to nod his head to indicate that he understood.

"Good, now that we have that established, we must get on about our business here." Jon slid the barrel of the Uzi from the technician's mouth and jerked him upward until the man was sitting up. "Where are the others?"

The technician tried to shake off his fear, but it didn't work. His voice trembled as blood dripped from his mouth onto his lab jacket. "I haven't been inside for over an hour. Last time I was in there, they were all in their quarters. What do you want?"

Jon slapped the man across the side of his face with the Uzi and almost knocked him from the counter. "I ask the questions, not you." Jon grabbed the tech's collar again and jerked him upright. More blood flowed from a large laceration on his face and streamed onto his jacket. Little white remained on the right side of the man's coat from the shoulders down.

The technician grabbed at the cut on his face and tried to slow the bleeding. He was feeling light-headed and weak. He knew he was bleeding profusely and he had to get it stopped or he would lapse into unconsciousness. He also knew he had to warn the others inside the laboratory, even though it would probably cost him his life.

"I like it so much more when you express a willingness to cooperate with me. Now, get back to your work station and enter the sequence necessary to clear the locks on the outer chamber doors. One digit out of place or one alarm, and I will decorate this place with your brains. Clear?"

The technician nodded.

Jon pressed the Uzi against the technician's ear when the guy sat back in the seat from which he had pulled him seconds earlier. "Now, slowly and deliberately do as I instructed you. Remember, behave as if your life depends on it . . . because it does."

The technician entered a program code and the outer door to the laboratory clicked.

Jon pointed toward the door with his free hand and the intruders who filled the reception room moved quickly to the door.

All but one.

Jon looked at the technician and then at the last intruder. He nodded his head and the hard-faced, armed man cleared the nylon sheath on his hip with a large tanto knife. In a move so calculated and fast that it defied the eye to see it, the man arched outward with the surgically sharp knife and raked it across the technician's throat before the startled tech could even gasp. The intruder smiled with satisfaction and wiped the bloody blade clean on the tech's lab jacket. He took one final look at his victim lying dead on the lab floor, wide-eyed, with a gaping incision where his Adam's apple had been only seconds before. Then he sheathed the knife and ran to catch the others, who had entered the security door in front of him.

Jon was already there. He stood at the door and looked at the fallen technician with undisguised apathy. Then he turned and faced his men who were huddled together in the hallway on the other side of the doorway. He glanced quickly at his watch. "On my mark, ten seconds. Secure the facility. Three, two, one . . . now!"

The armed insurgents dispersed silently and methodically in pairs throughout the laboratory.

The first team moved down a long white hallway illuminated by fluorescent lights. They stopped in front of a doorway marked by a small engraved nameplate. It read: TRUNK ROOM. They tried the doorknob, but the door was locked. One of the men fumbled for a few seconds with the tip of a fighting knife and the door sprang open. Both men rushed inside and immediately inspected small twisted pairs of wires. They selected the ones that were crucial first, and severed them from the main telephone trunk cable that fed through a three-inch metal conduit extending from the concrete floor. When they had rechecked their work, they identified the wire pairs that linked the laboratory alarm system to the main security control room across the compound. The taller of the men looked stone-faced at his companion. "Redundant. Two pairs each," he said.

His companion nodded and quickly retrieved two small aluminum boxes from his pack. Each box had a pair of wire leads that terminated in alligator clips. He laid them on the floor and grabbed a digital voltmeter from his pack. He attached the leads from the voltmeter to the termination block on the wall where the alarm lines from the trunk fed into the central control panel in an adjacent room. "Forty-eight volts. Twenty mils. Both pair. Perfect."

"Good," his companion replied.

The man let the voltmeter dangle at the end of the leads and grabbed both aluminum boxes from the floor. He attached one alligator clip to each side of the twisted pair and flipped a tiny toggle switch. A red LED came on and the small ammeter on the box indicated twenty milliamps. He did the same thing with the second box, attaching it to the redundant pair of wires feeding the alarm console. When the LED lit on that box, he took a pair of diagonal wire cutters from the pack and clipped all four wires that fed the main console in the laboratory. He doubled-checked his work and smiled. "This system is neutralized. We may proceed unimpaired by the outside world."

The other man pressed a small switch on his belt-mounted transmitter. "Neutralized. Proceed."

Outside in the main section of the laboratory, Jon nodded his head when he heard the radio report.

The underground facility came alive with the crashing sounds of doors bursting from their hinges and screams muffled by the roaring sounds of gunfire. The insurgents initiated a room-by-room search for inhabitants.

Jon spoke into his transmitter as he stood outside a door with an engraved nameplate that read PRIVATE. "Bring the woman to me. Terminate the rest of them." He motioned with his head and the two armed hardcases beside him kicked the door open. They rushed inside, weapons searching for a recipient of hot death.

Dr. von Wirth reached slowly for his glasses and turned deliberately in his swivel chair. He stared at Jon when he entered the room, flanked on each side by assault-rifle-bearing men. "You are the one called Jon, I presume?"

"Correct," Jon said. "And you are Dr. von Wirth?"

"I am." Von Wirth glanced at his wristwatch. "You are very prompt. I trust your efficiency is equal to your promptness."

Jon's expression grew instantly cocky. A slight smile parted his lips as he stepped forward and offered his hand to von Wirth in a gesture of goodwill. "Of that, sir, you may be assured. This facility is neutralized and under our control. We are ready to implement stage two."

The narrow grassy area surrounding the Marshall Space Flight Center mission control facility was dimly lit by a single mercury-vapor light at the northeast corner of the building. Two security guards drank coffee and played cards in a tiny office inside the east access door. They occasionally looked up and scanned closed-circuit television monitors that panned the hallways and access doors of the building.

Roger Spiker crouched low in the shabby shrubbery that lined the perimeter of the building. He looked through infrared binoculars into the darkened hallway outside the security office. He turned back to the insurgents behind him and motioned for them to stay down. Then he turned back to the doorway and stroked his scraggly beard as if it helped him contemplate his next move.

Spiker sat that way for over a minute. He glanced down at his left wrist and touched a button on the side of his watch that caused the digital face to light. His facial muscles tightened. Only thirty-seven seconds remained until showtime.

The roar of a diesel tractor shifting gears broke the

early-morning silence. Spiker raised his hand again and glanced back at the heavily armed men behind him. Then headlights swept across the grounds as the big diesel rig made a right turn onto the paved road beside the control center. The rig coasted to a stop and the driver climbed from the cab. The engine idled and sent puffy smoke into the night that was silhouetted against a mercury vapor light at the intersection behind it.

The driver, Todd Gallagher, walked to the double glass doors at the security facility and pressed the intercom button.

The speaker at the doorway came alive. "Security. Who's there?"

"Freight delivery," Gallagher said.

"What kind of delivery? We don't have anything showing on the schedule," the security guard replied through the intercom.

"Hey, I don't write the schedules. I just make the runs. My bill of lading says I got a control console in six pieces for delivery to the Marshall Space Flight Center. This is Marshall and this is the building. So what do you want me to do?"

"I can't clear you to enter. I'll need to check into it. Might be morning before I can get clearance," the guard said.

Gallagher was ready for the standard reply. "Well, might be morning for you, but come morning I plan to be sittin' at a truckstop in Birmingham drinkin' coffee. If you don't want this thing, I'm gonna drop it on the pavement out here and you can explain to the powers that be why it's outside instead of inside. Don't bother me none 'cause I'm gonna be long gone. It's up to you."

"Okay, what's your name?"

"Todd Gallagher."

"What freight lines?"

"Constellation," Gallagher said. He knew it was a lie when he said it, but none of that would matter in a few minutes.

"Who is your dispatcher?"

"Look, guys, I ain't gonna sit out here in the friggin' cold all night and wait while you sip coffee and play gin rummy. I'm gonna off-load this shit, and if you want it, come out and get it. Ain't my ass, you understand. I've met my destination. The rest of the problem is yours. Dispatcher's name is Herbert Henshaw. When you get him on the phone, you tell what I said I'm gonna do. He'll agree."

The voice through the speaker seemed a little more concerned. "All right, we're coming out to check the load. I got no idea where we'll put the thing, but we'll be out in a minute."

Gallagher looked through the glass doors and saw two flashlight beams bouncing side by side down the hallway toward the doors. He stood back and waited while the men opened the heavily locked doors.

"You Gallagher?" the guard asked.

Gallagher shook his head in disgust. "You see anybody else around here?"

"Sorry for the hassle. I'm Jim Bates and this is Tom Mosley. We had to hang in there with procedure. I hope you understand." Bates gestured toward Mosley and smiled.

Gallagher tried as best he could to act indignant. "Yeah, well, I've been drivin' all friggin' night and I ain't much on procedure. What do you want to do with this stuff?"

Bates motioned toward the trailer. "Can we take a look?"

"Hell, boy, I'll let you do one better than that. You can help unload it if you want to. Follow me."

Bates propped the door open. He and Mosley followed Gallagher toward the truck. Bates spoke while they walked. "I can't believe nobody told us about this. I guess it's just par for the course. Lowly security guards don't know anything about anything till it's already happened."

"You're right about that," Gallagher said. He spun around quickly. A silenced Ruger .22 automatic appeared in his hands and flashes of fiery death spat from the barrel. A pair of double-tapped CCI Stingers slapped Bates and Mosley almost simultaneously in the forehead. The instant trauma and the scorching hot lead instantly erased their lives.

# Chapter Five

□ □ □

Carl squeezed the firing mechanism the second he saw the first trail of fire. The Leeco rig trembled from the force of the LAR rocket launching from the port retractable pod. The infrared heat-seeking nose of the Leeco bird chewed through darkness and air until it locked electronically on the explosive bird teaming down on the cab of the high-tech rig. Halfway between the hovering chopper and the Leeco cab, a cyclonic explosion caused the earth to shake. A catastrophic orange fireball filled the cut slope in front of the cab, and for an instant, the chopper vanished from sight.

The pilot, Lonnie Albright, was a seasoned combat veteran at the stick of a Bell Jet Ranger helicopter. But he could never recall being counterattacked by an eighteen-wheeler equipped with antiaircraft artillery. In his mind, it just wasn't possible. He was stunned and unsure whether the explosion was caused by his death bird or some other unexplained reason. He sat hovering until the fire burned itself away enough for him to see the Leeco rig.

Carl fingered another LAR, this time from the starboard pod. Fire streaked through the night across the distance separating the rig and the chopper.

Albright was watching now, startled. He saw the streak of fire homing in on the nose bubble of his flying machine and he knew he had only one chance at survival. His moves were completely instinctive: he cut power, feathered the rotator, and let the bird drop toward the pavement fifteen feet away. The chopper descended below the crest of the rise in the highway and vanished from sight. The skybird slapped into the pavement, rocked hard, and settled to a jolting, bone-jarring stop. In the same instant, the Leeco LAR swished across the crest of the knoll and vanished with a trail into the darkness behind the whirlybird.

"He's good," Carl yelled. "Damn bird missed."

Marc fought the rig for control, purposely fishtailing from side to side in an evasion technique just in case the chopper reappeared. "He's done this crap a time or two."

"What next, bro?" Carl asked. His finger still rested on the firing mechanism while his eyes scanned the computer screen for any sign of his target.

Marc gritted his teeth, his voice low and controlled. "It's the Lee Law of Aircraft Physics as applied to helicopters in the middle of an interstate highway. What goes down must come up . . . or get shattered into pieces by a speeding high-tech overroad rig."

"I'm listening, bro, and I'm watchin' on the infrared scanner. He comes up anywhere out there in the darkness and I got the bead on him. One twitch of my finger and his Plexiglas bubble is popped forever."

"I like it. Let's nail this creep's ass."

"Roger, Colonel. You drive and I'll shoot," Carl said. His eyes never left the armament sight on the computer screen.

Marc grabbed a lower gear and crammed the accelerator to the floor. The 1400-horsepower diesel engine spat raw torque to the driveshaft and the rig leaped forward. Marc watched the highway and dodged as much burning debris from the rockets as he could. Carl kept his eyes on the screen and his finger perched at the ready on the firing mechanism.

The rig burst through the obstacle course of debris and churning black smoke. And then, like a monster appearing from a dark lagoon, it penetrated the other side of the smoke cloud at the top of the knoll where the chopper was hiding just beyond the crest. The rig's quartz-halogen headlights bored through the darkness and lit the chopper like daylight.

"Bingo!" Carl yelled.

The word had hardly cleared his throat when a swarm of angry, sizzling hornets streaked from the undercarriage of the chopper as it churned the air and tried to lift off. The 7.62mm death missiles chewed pavement in a lethal streak that headed straight for the Leeco rig. A string of glowing tracers lit the path of destruction intended for Marc and Carl.

Marc steered hard left to avoid the death spray. He was a fraction of a second too late. A torrent of the hellfire pelted the right side of the Leeco cab and riveted a pattern of wanton death along the side of the trailer. But the 7.62mm projectiles were no match for the Leeco machine's Armorshield coating. Their potentially fatal stings were harmlessly repelled by the state-of-the-art outer shell that encapsulated the rig.

Marc cut back to the right and straightened the rig. He kept the accelerator to the floor, the rig gaining momentum with each fraction of a second. He made a mental line to the front bubble of the Bell warbird.

The chopper's tail flipped left, then right as Albright fought the stick to get the bird to take air. Its rotors slashed air with increasing speed and the machine bounced on and off the pavement. His portable sun beneath the undercarriage had been crushed with the harsh landing seconds before. And now, all he could see was high-intensity white light bearing down on him at the front end of the Leeco rig. Albright crammed the throttle forward and gave the chopper everything it had. It lifted off the pavement, spun around, and took air. It wasn't the way he had wanted to leave the place, but under the emergency conditions, it would have to do. The chopper gained altitude and made a maddening effort to climb into the dark Virginia sky.

"He's going!" Marc yelled.

"Not far," Carl said confidently. He flipped the actuator for the laser sight and shot an electronic beam of light at the fleeing bird. He made mental calculations and pressed the firing switch. "Hellfire's coming, fly-boy."

A pair of laser tracking Hellfire missiles streaked from the Leeco rig with a thunderous roar. A blazing trail of fire marked the course to death and destruction.

A quarter mile in front of the rig, the night sky turned light with a cataclysmic burst of red, white, and orange fire that churned towers of black smoke into the atmosphere. The second explosion came a heartbeat after the first and then the fuel tanks filled with high-octane gasoline ruptured and exploded. The fiery remains of the helicopter plummeted to the earth with unforgiving, life-taking speed.

Carl lifted his finger from the firing trigger, a look of satisfaction relaxing his face. He glanced at Marc. "Top-secret mission, my ass!"

Marc slowed the rig as they approached the area where the helicopter disintegrated. "I think it's time to get on the horn and get an update on what the hell is going on here. Either we're two of the biggest patsies of all time, or the Pentagon has sprung a major leak. I want to know which and I want to know now. If I'm gonna take a chance on getting killed, I want to know just what it is I'm dying for."

"I second that," Carl said. He reached for the microphone attached to the Icom V-100 transceiver that would link him directly to Delta Force Command at the Pentagon in Washington via the ComSat-D orbiting satellite and the nationwide Defense Department radio repeater system. "I'm dying to know before I die."

Dr. von Wirth sat patiently at his lab counter while the insurgents searched the research facility. Jon sat at a small worktable near the doorway. His small radio transceiver sat on the table, the volume low. Two armed men stood by the door and watched the hallway for any scientists or research technicians that tried to flee.

Jon and von Wirth listened to the two-way radio while the scenario unfolded outside the room in the other areas of the lab. One by one, the rooms were searched and the inhabitants killed or captured. Minutes passed, and finally the report came to indicate complete neutralization of the facility.

Jon picked up the radio and pressed the transmit switch. "This is IU-two command. Status report."

The radio crackled. "IU-two, we have total neutralization. Thirteen captives including the woman. Fourteen confirmed dead. No IU casualties. Over."

Jon smiled, a look of satisfied accomplishment filling his rugged face. He spoke into the radio again. "Roger. Bring the woman to the front near the elevator. Take the others to the experiment chambers and secure them. Do not harm them. We will have need of them soon. Leave two men to watch them. Firearms are prohibited here, so they are harmless. Over."

"Affirmative," a voice replied over the radio.

Jon looked toward the guards at the doorway. One of them glanced back into the room. "Dennis, when they bring the woman from the residential quarters, bring her to me inside."

"Yes, sir," Dennis replied.

Von Wirth had sat motionless and silent. He shuffled in his chair and stared at Jon. "We must be sure everything is clear on the outside. This mission cannot be accomplished unless all personnel are in the proper positions. Timing is critical."

Jon turned around and looked hard at the old scientist. "You worry too much, doctor. We will be in complete control of the Marshall Space Flight Center within the next thirty minutes. Our personnel will be in every strategic location and we will let nothing stand in the way of successful completion of this project."

Voices outside the room stopped the conversation. Two insurgents moved swiftly through the hall toward von Wirth's office. They brought a woman with them. She was in her midthirties with shoulder-length brown hair and dressed in a thin pale blue nightgown. She struggled against the force of the two men who half carried and half dragged her through the hall. She cursed them, her head jerking violently from side to side as she struggled.

The men forced her through the doorway and stopped in front of the table where Jon sat. He turned slowly and deliberately around until he was facing her.

She froze.

Jon stared into the woman's light brown eyes, but he didn't speak. His face was hard and cold.

She remained still, her eyes fixed on his.

Jon's lips barely moved when he spoke. "You are a spirited one. Quite an admirable trait."

She didn't move or show any reaction.

Jon nodded to the guards. "Let her free. Wait outside and close the door behind you."

The men obeyed. They released her arms and she immediately rubbed them to get the circulation flowing again.

Jon forced an artificial smile. "You are Dr. Kathleen Caldwell?"

"You obviously know that or you wouldn't have asked. Of course I'm Dr. Caldwell." She jerked her head toward Dr. von Wirth. "Who are these people?"

Von Wirth didn't reply. Instead, he sat motionless in his chair and listened.

Jon stood and moved beside the table. "Perhaps I am better prepared to answer your questions. That will come in time. You are divorced. No children. You graduated from the University of Virginia with a bachelor's degree in science and a biology major. You attended graduate school at Vanderbilt University, where you obtained a masters in biology. You stayed in research there and completed your doctorate with a specialty in microbiological research. You have worked in this facility for seven years. You have been divorced for eight years. Your former husband holds a masters in business administration from Vanderbilt. He owns Caldwell Transportation Services in Fort Wayne, Indiana. He has never remarried, nor have you. Your husband is still very much in love with you even after the divorce. That makes you very valuable to me."

Caldwell stood firm. "I'm glad to see you have more than adequate resources for your research. I suppose you know what size diaphragm I use, too?"

"You don't use one," Jon said quickly. "You haven't had the need in several years."

Caldwell mellowed. "Okay, you've proven your point. Who are you and what do you want from me?"

"I am Jon. That is all you need to know now. I am the commander of these insurgents. We have taken control of this facility. We are the American Civilian Defense Movement and this, my dear, is a revolution."

Caldwell laughed. "I take it I should be impressed. Well, I'm not. What is it you want?"

Jon rested his hands on the table and peered into Caldwell's eyes. "I have what I want. I have you, Dr. von Wirth, and control of this facility. That means I have control of the neurological interrupter gases and the self-generating biological materials you have stored here. Your husband's love for you will give me what I need next."

Caldwell was getting restless now. She shifted her weight on her feet a couple of times and looked nervously at Jon. "Oh? And what might that be?"

"More transportation to assure final delivery of the horrible weapons matériel you have stored within this facility."

Caldwell stood straight and alert. Her voice was strong. "You can't be serious. You haven't any idea what the repercussions of your actions will be. Self-replicating biological viruses are capable of inducing sickness and death in millions of people once they are uncontained in the atmosphere. We have no known antidote. The antibody properties haven't been isolated. We are still in basic research and developmental stages. To remove these agents from the sterile confines of this laboratory is insane. It would be international genocide for humanity and suicide for you. Tell him, Dr. von Wirth. Explain to this homicidal maniac what he's talking about, what would happen if these experimental organisms were ever loosed on the atmosphere."

Von Wirth's brow raised and he started to speak, but Jon cut him off.

"My dear, Dr. Caldwell. Dr. von Wirth has already explained all of this to the people who initiated this mission. Why else would we be here?"

Caldwell jerked around and stared at von Wirth. "Doctor, tell me it isn't so."

Von Wirth nodded.

Caldwell shook her head in indignant dismay. "I don't believe it. This is absolute insanity. If you release even one of the dozens of viruses used in our research, the potential exists that in a matter of weeks there would be few if any, well survivors. What have you gained? If you destroy the people out there on the surface, you'll destroy yourselves also. You can't possibly understand the power of chemically induced neurological interruption or self-replicating viruses. We don't even know what might happen, really. What could you possibly stand to gain? Tell me, what?"

"Control," Jon said. "Total control."

Roger Spiker was the third man back from the point man when the insurgents moved into the master control section at the Marshall Space Flight Center. The armed man on the point rushed into the facility with the muzzle of his assault rifle sweeping and searching the area in front of him for a target. When he found none, he stopped at a hallway and motioned for the next man back to move.

Allen Sikes moved past the point man and ran low in a crouch to the security control room where the two now-dead guards had played cards only moments before. Sikes checked the television monitors first. He saw nothing unusual there, so he immediately shrugged his backpack from his shoulders and sat it on the floor. He laid his assault rifle on the desk on top of the playing cards left there by the dead guards.

Curiosity got the best of him. Sikes stared at the unplayed card hand lying facedown on the desk. He picked up the cards and flipped them over. "I'll be damned," he said. "A full house. Aces and eights . . . the dead man's hand."

Sikes dropped the cards back on the desk and continued his work. Another precautionary glance at the monitor bank. Still nothing there. He ripped open the Velcro top on his backpack and removed a half-dozen electronic gadgets. As he lined them up on the desk beside his rifle, Sikes briefly inspected each one. When he was satisfied that none of them had been damaged in transit, he removed a roll-up tool pouch from the backpack and moved to the monitor switching panel.

Sikes sat on the counter beside the switching rack and unrolled the tool pouch. He glanced at the screws on the panel and grabbed a Phillips screwdriver from the nylon holder inside the pouch, then made one more fast glance at the monitors to be sure there was no movement on them. There was none, so he slipped the screwdriver into the first of ten Phillips-head screws and removed it from the panel.

Five minutes passed until the last screw was unthreaded from the switching panel. Sikes lifted the heavy wire-mesh cover and pulled a AAA mini-MagLite from his shirt pocket. He twisted the head on the tiny flashlight and shined the beam on the components inside the switch box. When he located the wire jumpers he was looking for, he checked the monitors one more time, then slid the pin-terminated wires from their connectors.

Sikes moved quickly to the desk and grabbed six small electronic modules. Each module was less than one inch square and sealed in a body of hardened black epoxy. Three sets of twisted wire pigtails dangled from each of the small units. One set of wires terminated in pinned leads and the other two were pinned just like the wires he had disconnected inside the video switching box.

Sikes detected movement in his peripheral vision. He jerked around quickly, his right hand moving toward his assault rifle in the process. His eyes connected with the source of the movement at precisely the same instant his hand wrapped around the rifle.

"How's timing?" Roger Spiker asked when he stepped into the security room.

Sikes felt relief when he saw Spiker. He released the assault rifle and picked up another module. "Gettin' there, my man. You spooked the hell out of me. I didn't see you coming. Are we on schedule out there?"

"Like clockwork. Our people are in the main control room now. We should have the system compromised on schedule. Curly and Gentry are changing into the uniforms they took from the guards. They'll be in here in a few minutes. You got everything under control?"

Sikes moved back to the counter and the video switching box. He reached inside and connected the pigtails from the first module to the pins where he had disconnected the wires. "It's cool. Takes a little time, that's all. Five more minutes and I'm out of here."

Spiker scanned the security shack, scrutinizing the electronics that provided security for the Marshall Center mission control. Then he moved to the doorway. "Next stop, the uninterruptible power supply room. See you in six minutes at the UPS."

"I'll be there," Sikes said without looking up from his work. "This place makes me nervous. I'll be damned glad to get this finished, climb back in my rig, and get the hell away from Huntsville, Alabama."

"I second that," Spiker said. He swept the area

outside the room with the barrel of his assault rifle. Satisfied it was clear, he walked briskly away and down the hall.

Sikes continued to install the modules in the video switching control. When installation of the modules was completed, the video images displayed on the security monitors could be manipulated from a remote station inside one of the insurgent eighteen-wheelers parked inconspicuously near the water tower training unit on the back side of the space center compound. A simple flip of a switch and the guards would see whatever images were transmitted to them from the rig. All other images, the real ones from the security cameras, would be rerouted to electrical ground.

Three units to go. Sikes worked as quickly and as carefully as he could.

"Who are you and what are you doing here?"

The hard and mean voice came from behind Sikes. Startled, he jerked his hands free of the switching box. He turned and saw a man in a guard's uniform with a revolver pointed at him. And it wasn't Curly or Gentry.

He froze, staring at the man. And then the muzzle flash obscured his view.

# Chapter Six

□ □ □

Dermont Ashland bolted upright in the bed, his eyes open wide. He was trembling. Every muscle in his body was tight and throbbing. His hands held the sheets in a deathlike grip and his chest felt like someone was ripping a knife through it. Ashland took a deep breath and looked around the dark bedroom. It was only then that he realized the horrible vision that had awakened him from deep sleep had been nothing more than a bad dream. He moved his arms and felt the bed around him. It was wet, soaked. Then he realized he was sweating profusely. A cold, frightening sweat. And he knew it didn't end there. Something had gone wrong. He felt it in his bones.

Someone or something had discovered the insurgents at Marshall and all hell was about to break loose. Not just in Huntsville, but all over the country. Probably even the world. If the insurgents were discovered or something had gone astray before the perpetrators were in place, the potential repercussions were horrifying.

Ashland took a few more deep breaths and sat still. He gathered and organized his thoughts. Where could the plan fail? Even before the thought flashed completely through his mind, he knew the answer. It could fail anywhere along the line.

Ashland managed to move his right hand. He reached over to the oak nightstand beside the bed and fumbled for the switch on the lamp. He found it and moved the roller. The room lit immediately; Ashland squinted under the sudden burst of light. He looked at the telephone beside the lamp and contemplated making a call to Ramone. He knew that was a violation of the arrangement, but his fear and curiosity were getting the best of his reason.

He hesitated and looked carefully around the room. There were no hard-faced men with guns like there had been in the dream. There was no fire, gunfire, or screams. There was only silence. Ashland stared at the telephone. His usual decisiveness deserted him, he felt intimidated. But if the project hadn't gone astray, to breach safety and security would be a serious error. After all, telephone records were easily retrieved and readily admissible in criminal courts.

The telephone rang. Ashland stiffened even more and clutched his chest with both hands.

It rang again.

Ashland's eyes were fixed on the beige phone. His heart raced and he felt perspiration pouring from his skin.

The third ring sounded.

Ashland managed to make his right arm move. He stopped with his hand almost touching the receiver.

Then the fourth ring came.

Ashland picked the receiver up. "Yes," he said nervously.

"We must talk," Ramone said coldly.

"In the morning," Ashland replied.

"Now." Ramone's voice hardened. "We have encountered some difficulty. It must be discussed now."

"What time is it?"

"Two-ten."

"But—" Ashland said.

Ramone interrupted. "No but's. I must see you now. Immediately."

"Where?" Ashland asked.

"You come here or I will come there. You choose," Ramone replied.

"I don't like either option. Isn't there a neutral place where we won't arouse curiosity?"

"You tell me," Ramone said.

"There is a small conference room at the ATS terminal. We can get in there at this time of morning. I use it frequently for late meetings. I'm not very fond of going there without prior notice. Are you sure this can't wait?"

"Sure, it can wait if you don't want to be a free man this time tomorrow. It's your decision. I'll cover my backside either way. If I don't like the way it falls, I'll be on a plane out of this country before the sun comes up. Make a decision."

Ashland felt a drop of sweat strike his chest as it fell from his brow. He breathed deeply and then sighed. "ATS in twenty minutes. Do you have transportation?"

Ramone sounded relieved. "Yes. Twenty minutes at ATS. I'll be there."

The telephone line clicked back to a dial tone and Ashland laid the receiver back into the cradle. He sat staring blankly at the walls for a long moment, his face flushed and pale. Then he returned to reality, ripped the covers back, and climbed from the bed. After an obligatory stop in the bathroom, he went to his closet and fumbled for his clothes.

Ashland dressed quickly in a two-piece suit and tie. He stood in front of the mirror and combed his hair.

When he was finished, he went back to the bathroom and brushed his teeth.

Satisfied with his appearance, Ashland went back to his clothes closet and dug through a stack of shoe boxes. He found the one he wanted and lifted the lid. Inside lay a dull-finished revolver. Ashland picked it up, swung the cylinder open to verify it was still loaded, closed the cylinder, and slid the weapon inside his pants at the small of his back.

Insurance.

Ashland walked back to the bed and sat down. He looked at the telephone again and his mind raced. He couldn't make a decision. Security had already been breached and he questioned his judgment about further breaching it. He knew he should make the call, but he decided against it. Instead, he made up his mind to wait until the meeting with Ramone was over. When that was finished, he could call and give a full update. It was very important to keep everyone abreast of new developments.

Ashland pressed the red button on the intercom beside the telephone to page Howard in his first-floor sleeping quarters.

"Yassir?" Howard asked sleepily.

"Howard, I have been called to a very important meeting. Have the car ready in five minutes."

"Right, sir," Howard replied.

"Thank you, Howard," Ashland replied. He cleared the intercom and stared once more at the telephone. Without hesitation, he picked up the receiver and pressed the buttons until the number he sought rang on the other end.

"Okay," the cold answering voice said.

"Frank," Ashland said, "potential problem. ATS in fifteen minutes. I'll already be there with our boy. I think we should accelerate the program. When I leave, take care of it."

"Something amiss?" Frank asked.

"Apparently. I have nothing more. When acceleration is complete, we can discuss it. The potential is great for an abort and evacuation. If that becomes necessary, initiate *dirty pool*."

"I understand," Frank replied, accepting the code name for the security plan designed to ensure that no ends were left dangling . . . unless at the end of a taut rope.

"I have no word on integrity of the pie," Ashland said, referring to the Marshall Space Flight Center. "Perhaps I will know more when I visit the baker."

"Excellent," Frank said. "Hopefully we have equitable slices."

"Yes. Just be sure acceleration is completed. Should I meet with misfortune, you know the letter of my wishes."

"Yes, sir."

"Don't be late," Ashland said, and he laid the receiver back into the cradle. He turned around toward the door to leave and saw Ramone standing in the doorway.

Dermont Ashland froze and the dream started all over again. Only this time, it was real.


"Barnburner, this is Pathfinder. Do you copy? Over." Carl lowered the microphone, checked the channel display on the Icom. He waited patiently for a response from either Delta Force Command inside the Pentagon in Washington, or Brittin Crain at FBI headquarters in downtown D.C.

"Everybody must be catching a little nap," Marc said. He steered the Leeco rig south on I-81 without regard to traffic police or other interference. "At this hour of the morning, who can blame them?"

"Yeah, I second that," Carl replied. "With the welcoming committees we've encountered in the last few miles, I'm beginning to wish I'd slept tonight, too."

"Hit 'em again," Marc said. "I heard the squelch tail from the bird, so it's working okay."

Carl pressed the push-to-talk switch on the side of the black Icom noise-canceling microphone and held it inches from his mouth. "Barnburner, this is Pathfinder. Do you copy on Echo uplink of ComSat-D? Over."

"Huh," Marc said. "Strange. We've never had that problem before. Give 'em a try via packet through the uplink and send it down on the November downlink. That should bring it out in the face of the console operator at DFC. Unless he's asleep or blind, it'll jump out at him. Tag a priority flag on it to get his adrenaline pumping."

Carl mumbled something unintelligible as the Leeco rig ate the night and white lines streaked by in a virtual solid line. "I don't use the packet mode often enough to remember how. You may have to coach me through it. Can you do that and drive?"

"No problem," Marc replied. "Display channel twelve on the Icom. That should take you into the transverter channel on the repeater. Hit U-L-T-A on the keyboard to energize the terminal node controller and bring up the transmitter. That will take the signal through the network backbone until it finds an earth station and it'll go up to the bird on the Alpha uplink. When the computer screen shows a lock on the bird, punch in our ID on the keyboard and route the path. I'll show you how when you get that far."

"Yeah, I remember the path. I can get that," Carl said. He pressed the correct keys and the transmit indicator appeared on the Icom display and the computer screen.

"While the machine is looking, bring up the auxiliary receiver from the trailer on the console speaker. Put it on channel one in the event somebody heard the call and answers us on FM voice." Marc glanced at the computer screen, but quickly focused on the taillights dotting the dark highway ahead.

Carl made the adjustment and turned the volume control up on the console auxiliary speaker.

Marc took a deep breath and sighed. "Something is really afoul here, bro. I wonder what other valiant interceptors we have waiting on down the road."

"No tellin'," Carl said as he stared at the computer screen, waiting for the uplink lock indicator. "Remember the time we did the deal in Central America? The senator's daughter, I think it was. Anyway, this reminds me of that disaster. If you recall, it was all hush-hush. One of those need-to-know-basis deals. Everybody and his damned cat knew we were comin' and where we were goin'. We were the last to know. That deal was screwed up from the beginning just like this one. Damn near got us killed, too."

"I remember. You never forget something like that. Politics at work. I certainly want more information on this baby-sitting job. From where I sit, everything is suddenly coming across very distorted. There's more to this run than we're being told. I hope whatever the reason is, it's a damned good one."

"It always is to the one who makes the decision. After all, it's not his ass on the hot seat. It's real easy to do stupid things when the muzzle ain't pointed at you. Armchair quarterbacks rank high on my top-ten list of people to dislike."

The computer chirped and flashed a message to indicate an uplink/downlink lock.

"What now?" Carl asked.

"Tell 'em to answer the damned radio. I want to talk to General Rogers and Brittin Crain."

Carl typed in the message and hit the transmit key. The indicator illuminated again and transmitted the signal into the nationwide Defense Department repeater network.

Seconds passed and a message appeared on the screen: *Activating Echo uplink for voice com. Please respond*.

The auxiliary speaker chattered. "Pathfinder, this is Barnburner. Do you have traffic? Over."

"Switch back to channel one on the Icom," Marc said.

Carl hit the channel-up button and the backlit digital display counted through channel sixteen and rolled to channel one. He picked up the microphone and pressed the transmit switch. "Barnburner, this is Pathfinder. We need direct contact with General Rogers or Brittin Crain. Top priority. Over."

The operator's voice crackled through the Icom speaker. "Roger, Pathfinder. We'll have to issue a priority page. Neither the general nor Agent Crain is present in the command center. Over."

"Can you give me a time estimate?" Carl asked.

The radio operator at DFC responded quickly. "We're keying the page now. Shouldn't be more than a few minutes. We may have to do a phone patch, but I can handle that from here. Over."

"Affirmative," Carl said. "The sooner the better. We're up to our butts in alligators out here."

"Affirmative," the operator said. "Stand by on this

channel. As soon as I have the word, I'll get back to you. Over."

"Roger, Barnburner. Pathfinder standing by." Carl slid the microphone back into its holder clip and glanced at the computer screen. He looked up at the road and the taillights marking the highway ahead. "You know, it's gonna be a long haul to Huntsville."

"Roger that," Marc said. He steered the rig and watched the road illuminated in the headlights of the Leeco rig. Every few seconds, he scanned the rearview mirrors out of habit. "I'm not real sure what we're into here. We've had two hitters in a very short period of time. Somebody from somewhere wants something we've got. Might be our asses or it could be that nuclear whatchamacallit in the vault of the trailer. Whatever it is, I'm not real happy about our unsociable guests."

"Let's assess this," Carl said. "Two hitters. One eighteen-wheeler and a chopper. What does that tell you?"

"Tells me whoever is behind this has a tubful of money to piss down the chute. That tells me they want whatever they're after real bad. I think there'll be more company before we get to Huntsville."

"Affirmative. Tells me something else."

"What's that?" Marc asked.

"Tells me we might be in for more of the same stuff when we get to the Space Flight Center. The Boss said we have to baby-sit that contraption twenty-four hours a day. If it's the reactor they're after, they not gonna be real thrilled if we get to Huntsville and they haven't gotten the goods. If it's trouble they want, nothing will stop them. We've been there before."

Marc glanced into the left rearview mirror. "We may be there again," he said excitedly.

"What?" Carl asked. He jerked his head left and looked at Marc in the ambient light of headlights.

Marc swiveled his head between the roadway in front of him and the left mirror. "Hot dog coming up fast in the go-faster lane. Activate the weapon systems. Here it comes again."

Allen Sikes dropped to the floor when the shot was fired. He saw the smoke from the barrel, but he wasn't sure he ever heard the sound. He was too scared. He frantically fumbled for his assault rifle, but he was far too late.

"It pays to watch your backside," Roger Spiker said.

Sikes managed to get up from the floor and dust himself off. "Man, I thought I was dead. Where'd he come from?" Sikes asked, pointing to the body of the dead guard on the floor.

"Beats me," Spiker said. "I was headed down the hallway when I heard him walking from the other direction. I just played a hunch that he was coming here. I knew if he found you before you knew he was there, well, the party was over."

"Wow. I'm sure glad you saw the turkey. He would have nailed my ass before I ever knew what happened. I owe you one."

"Pay me later. We have a job to do and a mission to accomplish," Spiker said. He leaned down to the dead guard's body and removed a service revolver from dead fingers. "I hope we don't find ourselves looking down the barrel of any more surprises like this one. Watch your backside. I'm going to the control center and be sure all conversions are on schedule."

"Yeah," Sikes said. He felt a chill rush through his body as he fully comprehended how close he had come to death. "I thought intelligence recon said there were only two guards on this shift."

"Right," Spiker said. He turned around and checked the hallway once more to ease his nerves. "Intelligence recon people ain't here to get their asses shot off. Let this be a lesson for you. It's a lot easier to plan a battle than it is to fight one. When you're pushin' paper and a pencil in the safety of an office somewhere, nobody's gonna kill you. Hell of a difference."

Sikes found himself still stunned from the shooting. He glanced at the television switch and then back at Spiker. "Thanks again. How's time?"

"We're rollin' on sched. If the guys in the control center are movin' all right, this is a done deal." Spiker slung his M-16 over his right shoulder on its sling and grabbed the dead guard by the feet. "I'll send somebody up from control to watch until you're finished in here. What's your completion time?"

"Five to seven minutes if my hands stop shaking," Sikes said.

"I'm out of here," Spiker said, and he started dragging the body from the guard shack.

"What are you gonna do with him?"

"Same thing we did with the others. Drop his dead ass in the chemical truck and close the lid before he starts turning to yucky goo. That shit eats 'em up in minutes. It's some kind of potent liquid, I'm tellin' you."

Sikes turned his head in disgust. Despite his generally unsociable demeanor, he still felt his stomach turn slightly at the mention of dropping a body into a tank truck full of flesh-devouring chemicals. "I'll get this done as fast as I can. I'd appreciate the backup from downstairs. I guess you're right, it's a hell of a lot different when it's your ass sizzlin' on the fryin' pan. That dead dude sure changed my attitude about life."

Spiker nodded and dragged the body to the double glass doors where two men from outside met him.

Sikes turned back to the television switch and continued connecting the twisted wires from the small electronic modules to the pins he had cleared minutes earlier. He worked hard and fast, but he still noticed his hands shaking each time he tried to push one of the pins down on the soldered posts. His nerves made him turn every ten or fifteen seconds to check behind him. With each check, he also scanned the closed-circuit television monitors to be sure there was no movement in any place where there shouldn't be.

There was none.

Sikes continued the installation of the modules. Two units remained to be installed, and then he heard footsteps in the hallway. He let the module drop from his hands into the switching cabinet. He dropped to his knees and grabbed the assault rifle on the table beside his tool pouch.

The steps grew closer and Sikes held the rifle with the safety off and ready. He directed the muzzle toward the hallway and waited for a target to appear in the doorway.

It did.

"Damn," Sikes said as he released the backward pressure on the trigger. "I'm glad it's you."

"Damn, dude, you're as punchy as a black man at a Klan picnic. Relax, get on with your work," the insurgent said.

"Yeah, if my hands ever stop trembling." Sikes shook his head to express his dissatisfaction with the plan. "Planning, my ass. You're Peterson, right? The South Carolina kid?"

"I'm the South Carolina dude. Greenville, actually. Hell of a nice place to live. Actually, I spent the first twenty years of my life in Manhattan. I like the foothills better," Peterson said. He turned back and checked the hallway, glanced at the double glass doors, and then turned back to Sikes.

"Great," Sikes said. "You make sure somebody doesn't come in and punch little round holes in my body and I'll get this shit finished and we're out of here. How's progress in the control room?"

"It's cool. They're wiring in the charges and the circuit bypass units similar to what you're doing. If somebody doesn't get a wire in the wrong place at the wrong time, they should be finished in fifteen minutes and we can split this creepy place. Shouldn't be a big deal, they're following the intelligence people's diagrams."

Sikes didn't say anything, but he shot a hard look at Peterson. Right now, the intelligence people's credibility was substantially diminished in his mind. He looked at the television switch and continued with his work.

"Can you believe it," Peterson said, "a place as critical to the manned space program as this and there are only three guards on duty at any one time?"

"That's government at work. Hell, boy, that's why we're doin' this. 'Cause of what the government's done to screw this country up. I ain't got no great loyalty to them Central American heathens. I'd just soon we kill all them, too. I just don't trust 'em."

Sikes picked up the last module and set it inside the switch console. He grabbed the twisted pair dangling from the black epoxy and reached for the vacant pins on the PC board.

The building shook with a violent tremor. Peterson dropped down, partly out of instinct and partly from the concussion. Black smoke and tongues of fire licked through the hallway and he choked and struggled for breath.

Sikes grabbed his ears and fell flat. The second explosion came and rocked the floors until they buckled outside the guard shack. And the third one came. And a fourth, and he couldn't hear anything except the ringing in his ears and the pain inside his head. All he could see was fire and smoke and his life flashing in front of his blinded eyes.

# Chapter Seven

□ □ □

The earth shook and trembled. Jon almost fell from his chair. The fluorescent lights inside the underground laboratory flickered, dimmed, and then relit to full intensity.

"What the hell was that?" Jon shouted.

Dr. von Wirth stood from his seat and moved around the lab. "Sometimes, when the research scientists and engineers are running test firings on the space-shuttle rocket engines, the earth will tremble like that. But at this hour, no. And not to this magnitude. There would be no conceivable reason for a test firing at this hour of the day. Besides, there is always a warning when a test is about to be initiated. The surface of the earth above us has suffered a massive trauma."

"What?" Jon asked. His facial color was fading and he felt himself growing weak-kneed. "Translate that."

Von Wirth ran his wrinkled fingers through his white hair. His face expressed how disgruntled it made him to repeat an explanation. "Something of substantial proportions has ignited or exploded on the surface somewhere in or around this facility."

"Could it possibly injure the structural integrity of this facility?" Jon asked. Deep inside, he wasn't really sure he wanted to know the answer to the question even before he asked it.

"Anything is possible, my friend. Anything is possible."

Dr. von Wirth moved back to his seat and sat down. He propped both elbows on the table in front of him and sat that way for a long moment.

"How many exits are there from this tomb?" Jon asked.

"One. The elevator shaft used for entry. There are no others that I am aware of and I have spent most of my life in this laboratory. I know it, every nook and cranny."

"Should we check the elevator and be sure it works?" Jon asked. His voice reflected his serious concern for his personal safety.

"Why?" von Wirth asked. "If it is still functional, we have no problem. If it isn't, why should any of us be concerned? We are here, five hundred feet below the earth's surface. There is nothing we can do to remedy our plight if we are stranded."

Dr. Caldwell had been silent. She had grown accustomed to the trembling earth in her years beneath its surface. She looked at the doorway and then at Jon. "Dr. von Wirth, I suggest we examine the integrity of the containment canisters and the culture mediums in the other experiment rooms. I don't recall a tremor as violent as this one. If they have incurred damage, we could have a problem."

Jon looked at her and didn't speak.

Von Wirth peeked through his hands and looked at Dr. Caldwell. "Yes, good thought. Have one of the technicians examine them."

"Maybe I would if there were any still alive. Your pal seems to have exterminated them."

"Yes, that's right," von Wirth said. "Hmm, a problem."

"What the hell are you people talking about?" Jon demanded.

"Perhaps you don't know as much about this center as you should, Jon. We have a large warehouse section in the rear of the laboratory. We also have a number of research and development labs for testing and culture of various chemicals and bacteria. If the tremor caused enough vibration, some of the chemicals or deadly bacteria cultures could have escaped into our synthetic atmosphere. Some of the bacteria are self-generating. All they need is moisture."

Jon was nervous. "So we don't let them get any moisture."

Dr. Caldwell said, "It isn't that simple. You see, there is sufficient moisture inside your lungs to cause the bacteria to multiply at astronomical speeds. You breathe it, it mixes with the liquids in your lungs, and you die. That's what we are all about here—death. A man of your profession shouldn't be afraid of a thing so simple as death. After all, it is just a mere biological function. We'll all be faced with it someday. Are you afraid, Jon?"

Jon was on his feet. He grabbed the front of Dr. Caldwell's nightgown and jerked her forward until his face was an inch from hers. In the same motion, his right hand shoved the barrel of his semiautomatic pistol into her temple. "Are you afraid of it, American bitch?"

Dr. Caldwell smiled. "Not at all, tough man. I've lived with death every day of my life for years. Don't forget, it's what I do for a living . . . I manufacture death."

Jon's lips were trembling. "I should blow your brains all over this room."

"Go ahead, kill me. I'm not scared. But before you

do, you'd better think about something. I'm the only one left here that's sane enough to make adequate determinations whether or not we have a leak. Kill me, and if there is a leak, you're dead, too. You'll feel fine until your lungs won't take any more air and you suffocate while your body drowns in its own fluids. So if that's what you want, go ahead. Pull the trigger."

Jon's hands were trembling now. The barrel of the pistol rested unsteadily on Dr. Caldwell's head. "Check the labs and the storage," he shouted into her face. "But when this is done and you have served your usefulness, I'm going to kill you myself. And that is a promise."

"I'm not afraid, tough guy," Dr. Caldwell said. "Death to me is just another part of living."

Jon jerked the pistol away and came across with his left hand open. It connected with Dr. Caldwell's face and caused her to lose her balance. She stumbled back and slammed into the wall. Blood trickled from her open mouth as she grabbed at the stinging, burning pain in her face.

Jon looked hard at her while she wiped the trickling blood from her lips. "I have made you a promise. I intend to keep it just as I intend to complete this mission. Nothing . . . understand me . . . nothing will stop the completion of this mission."

Dr. von Wirth watched in total apathy, as if nothing out of the ordinary was happening. His eyes looked and they saw. But whether his tired, old mind comprehended the magnitude of the potential problem was debatable. "Jon, we have much to attend to if we are to make the deadline. Let this incident rest."

"I'll let it rest," Jon said angrily. "I want this woman to understand that nothing will stop this mission and nothing will stop me from killing her. Nothing."

Dr. Caldwell straightened herself against the wall.

Fire came from her eyes as hate seared into Jon's. "You foolish bastard, maybe something already has stopped it. We may all be walking around in our tomb . . . at least until our food and energy supplies are interrupted or exhausted. When that happens, we won't be walking anymore. Think about it, Jon. Comforting, isn't it? Are you afraid?"

"You look unpleasantly surprised," Ramone said.

Ashland couldn't speak for a long moment. He stood there and stared at Ramone. When he finally found the strength to speak, he knew his voice exposed his fear. "You shouldn't have come here, Ramone. It is a violation of security and of our initial agreement."

"Screw security. This project has escalated far beyond the reaches of simple security."

Ashland choked more words from his throat, but he knew the fact that he hadn't moved a single step belied his attempt at an arrogant posture. "How did you get here so quickly? You were just on the telephone a few minutes ago."

Ramone's face remained expressionless. He reached into his coat pocket and produced a white portable cellular telephone. "I was already in the neighborhood and thought I'd stop by. I almost waited for you to leave so I could follow you. Then I got to thinking and I decided to save you a trip. Hope I'm not inconveniencing you at this late hour of the morning."

"How did you get in here without encountering Howard?" Ashland asked.

"I did encounter Howard."

"Why didn't he call me then?" Ashland paused and the probable answer ran through his mind. He gasped when the logical explanation occurred to him. "Did you harm him?"

Ramone put the cellular telephone back into his coat pocket. He stared hard into Ashland's eyes. "Only as much as was necessary."

"You bastard!" Ashland shouted. "There was no need. Howard was totally harmless. He presented no danger to you."

"I don't like loose ends," Ramone said.

"And what is that supposed to mean?"

"Howard. You. You're both loose ends. This mission has gone off course. I won't be here when the dust settles. Nor will you, for that matter."

Ashland felt his knees weaken. He knew he had to talk hard and fast if there was any chance of getting out of this situation alive. "What is the meaning of this insanity? I hired you and your people to do a job. Nothing more, nothing less."

Ramone was steadfast. "You hired me for a job. Money. I accepted for the good of my country. Your money is worthless to me. My interest lies solely in the nuclear reactor and the benefits its technology can yield to my country. For your money, I would not die. For the reactor and my country, I would die gladly. That is my purpose."

Ashland kept talking. "Your valiant purpose is admirable. I knew you were a dedicated man when I hired you. What is this problem you spoke of when you decided to breach the security of this project?"

"What difference does it make to you? You must know by now that I am going to kill you."

"I should have the consolation of knowing what went astray. This mission has been years in planning. There are people involved that you know nothing about. These people will not let my death go unnoticed. They will seek the answers. When they open this sordid can of worms, your country will surely suffer. They will hide the true nature of this project and avenge my death with the blood of your countrymen. Is that what you want?"

"No one will ever know I existed. There can be no retribution directed toward my country if I never existed, can there?"

Ashland forced a frightened, sarcastic smile. "You fool. Do you honestly believe I haven't shared your name, everything about you, with the people who are associated with me in this project? I may be old, but I am not senile."

Ramone revealed his first sign of weakening when his face took on a puzzled look. His left arm had been hanging casually by his side. He lifted it and placed his left hand in his coat pocket. "You're bluffing. Perhaps I should kill you now."

Ashland forced a laugh now and switched on the charm that had made him a multimillionaire. For the first time since the nightmare had awakened him, he felt he might have a chance at surviving the night. "Oh, no. You're the one who's bluffing because you know I'm telling you the truth. Perhaps we should call this a Mexican standoff and go into my den and talk about the problem that lit your fuse in the first place. Fighting each other will solve nothing. Together, perhaps we can overcome this problem. What do you say?"

Ramone stood firm, hand in pocket, his face uncertain. He knew he was in too deep to run and leave the old man alive. He also knew Dermont Ashland was a man who always stacked the cards in his favor, so it stood to reason that he had built in numerous safeguards to protect himself. That being the case, perhaps it was time to settle down, listen to the old man, and negotiate. "Perhaps we should."

"Good," Ashland said, "I have known you were a man of reason since I first met you. Shall we go?"

Ramone shifted his left hand in his pocket and stepped out of the doorway. "After you," he said, and gestured toward the hallway with his right hand.

Ashland found the strength to make his legs move. He walked to the door, looked hard at Ramone, and proceeded down the hallway. When he reached the long spiral staircase at the end of the hall, he stopped and looked at Ramone again. "Where is Howard?"

"Near the back of the house. Don't trouble yourself, old man. He's not dead, but he will have a terrific headache when he awakens."

Ashland breathed a sigh of relief and moved down the steps. When he reached the bottom of the huge foyer, he walked left toward the back of the house and then turned to his left again into a large room lined with bookcases. Ramone was directly behind him. Ashland stopped in front of a sofa and gestured toward a chair opposite it. "We can be comfortable here. Now, tell me about this problem."

Ramone sat down and looked carefully around the room. When he was satisfied that no harm would befall him, he spoke. "We have been forced to deal with incompetence."

"What do you mean?" Ashland asked as he tried to relax on the sofa.

"My men were running according to plan by following the truck carrying the reactor to Huntsville. They were waiting for the truck to stop somewhere and then they were to steal it. But then your men in the other truck and some fool you sent in a military helicopter attacked this truck making the haul. They blew it. The men in the truck you sent and the helicopter pilot are all dead. I have ordered my people to stay back until they deem the time right to overtake the men in the mule truck."

Ashland felt the blood draining from his face again. "What? How can this be? Are your men absolutely sure they have the correct truck?"

"Positive. There is no question about it. They have followed this truck since it picked up the reactor at the Pentagon in Washington, D.C."

Ashland made no attempt to hide his shock. "How can this possibly be?"

"Suppose you tell me that one. You're the one with all of the connections. Your people and you planned this operation. My Central American friends and I want only the reactor. I have no interest in this purpose you have selected. Our mission was to steal the reactor before it was transported into outer space. The Huntsville business and all of those chemical and biological weapons is your concern. I agreed to get them out of the laboratory and turn them over to you. What you do then is your business." Ramone shifted his weight in the chair and waited for Ashland to answer.

Ashland pondered the situation. "Why is it that armed men in a truck and a military helicopter cannot stop a single tractor-trailer?"

"My men said this truck is different. It is armed with all sorts of weapons. It destroyed your truck and the helicopter with its onboard firepower. Something is badly amiss, old man."

"Strange," Ashland said. He ran his fingers through his white hair and lost himself in a moment of deep thought. "I have never heard of an eighteen-wheeler in this country, or anywhere else for that matter, that is equipped with weapons. It doesn't make sense unless it is something the military has designed and built without the public's knowledge. Even so, to use an armed rig on America's highways is very strange. Someone in my planning unit would have surely known about it. You are sure there is no mistake about this?"

"No mistake," Ramone said defensively.

"Then we have a unique problem," Ashland said. "We must find out who these men are in this truck and to whom it belongs. Is the facility at Huntsville secured by your men and those other people we hired?"

"Yes. My last contact was . . ." Ramone paused and looked down at his wristwatch that was barely visible near the edge of his coat pocket where his left hand still rested. "Yes, twenty minutes ago. Everything was in place at that time."

"And your men are still following the initial plan?" Ashland asked.

"Yes. They will secure the materials from the laboratory, turn them over to your men, and leave. When they leave, everything will be in place and the Marshall control center will be wired for either destruction or takeover via your pirate radio signals. It is just according to plan. My next contact with them will be tomorrow evening on San Andres Island off the coast of Nicaragua. I want to be out of this country before dawn and I want that reactor with me when I leave. What happens after that is your problem. I will have fulfilled my obligation to you and your madness."

"Then I guess that makes you dispensable, doesn't it?" A cold voice near the doorway asked.

Ramone spun around and tried to get his pocket pointed in the direction of the door. He fired a single shot from the revolver tucked neatly in the pocket. The shot missed.

Frank rolled inside the room onto the floor. He fired twice from a large automatic pistol.

Ramone was on the floor, rolling now. He tried to jerk the revolver free from his pocket. It stuck.

Frank fired again and the first of two hot sizzling .45 hardballers struck Ramone in the shoulder. He catapulted backward and cursed through tightly clenched teeth.

Ramone got the revolver free and came around toward Ashland, who had frantically tried to get over the back of the sofa. He squeezed the trigger, but before the hammer dropped, a single shot from Frank's .45 auto sent a scorching 230-grain hardball into his head. Ramone's body quivered and his muscle reaction completed the trigger pull. His shot went wild into the ceiling and his lifeless body collapsed to the floor at Ashland's feet.

Frank was up now, the auto at arm's length and pointed straight at Ramone's head. He walked toward him and held the big gun steadily in a two-hand grip. When he was satisfied that Ramone was indeed dead, he let the auto drop to his side in his right hand and looked at Ashland. "Are you okay?"

Ashland was deathly pale and trembling. "Yes . . . yes, I am. How did you know?"

Frank smiled. "Instinct. It comes with the turf I call a playground. I learned a long time ago to never trust a foreign mercenary. Especially a radical one with a so-called *purpose*."

"Did you see Howard?" Ashland asked.

"Yeah, he's in the kitchen out back with an ice pack on his head. He'll be okay."

Ashland took deep breaths and tried to calm his shattered nerves. "We have to get him out of here and clean this mess. We have a lot to do if we're going to complete this project on schedule."

"Let's get on with the program," Frank said. He tucked the .45 into his waistband and leaned over toward

Ramone's body. Then he heard a safety click and he jerked upright.

Six men with weapons aimed were standing inside the large room. "No, no," one of the men said when Frank started to make a move for his weapon. "Do it and I'll splatter your brains all over this room. Don't even blink your eyes."

Frank stopped.

Ashland felt his knees weakening again and he gasped for breath.

The man aimed his automatic at Ashland. "Jefferson Dermont Ashland, we're the FBI and you are under arrest. Both of you. Place your hands over your heads and interlace your fingers, palms toward me. Do it now!"

# Chapter Eight

□ □ □

The speeding car was near the rear of the Leeco trailer. Marc clutched the steering wheel, ready to do battle.

"Weapons systems up and ready," Carl shouted. "Cameras on, videotape rolling, CAS engaged, auto acquisition engaged, infrared sights tracking the bandit on the left . . . standing by."

"He's coming on hard," Marc shouted. "No sign of hostiles yet."

"Got it," Carl replied. He watched the video display as the electronic sight moved with the speeding car coming up hard on the left side of the Leeco rig. His finger rested on the firing mechanism for the Stinger miniguns mounted in the cowling of the big diesel tractor.

"Midway now," Marc yelled.

"I got him on the screen. Let him take his best shot," Carl replied. "I've had about enough of this crap for one night."

The speeding car was nearing the rear of the tractor now. The sound of its roaring engine vibrated off the side of Marc and Carl's war machine. The occupants were visible now—two men, both in the front seat.

"Can't tell if they're hitters or not," Marc said. He alternated his glances at the highway and the speeding car. "Nothing yet."

"Still tracking," Carl shouted.

The taillights of the car became visible now and then the speeding machine rolled ahead of the Leeco rig. Marc made a mental note of the vehicle's license number and the state of registration.

"Maybe we're just nervous," Marc said, gradually reducing his alert threshold.

"Got damn good cause to be nervous," Carl said. He kept his eyes on the screen while the advanced electronic sighting system tracked the speeding car. The sight appeared on the CRT display as a circle about the size of a dime. Inside the circle was a flashing red $X$. As the target moved, the sight moved with it, and all the while the barrels of the deadly Stinger miniguns tracked in unison. At the touch of his finger, Carl could unsheath a death fusillade that would be all but impossible for the occupants of the car to survive.

"Strange," Marc said. "I would have bet that character was a hitter. He came from out of nowhere and he was bearing down on us like a bat out of hell."

"I still don't like it," Carl replied. "Might be something to it. He's in front now. Could give him a golden opportunity to ambush us down the superslab. I say we keep the systems up and our eyes open until we've gone on down the road for a while. What do you think?"

"Affirmative," Marc replied. "Shit can still happen."

The Icom speaker blared. "Pathfinder, this is Barnburner. Do you have traffic?"

"Answer the good general," Marc said. His eyes were still scanning the highway while the Leeco rig chewed asphalt and spat out white lines behind them.

"Roger, Barnburner, this is Pathfinder. We got a little problem on this run. Over."

"Affirmative, Pathfinder. We have a few problems on this end also. We just received a teletype from mission control in Houston. They have lost all digital communications with the control center in Huntsville. Since my page from DFC, we have learned of a massive explosion at Marshall. What's taking place from your end? Over."

Carl keyed the Icom microphone and spoke. He kept his eyes locked on the computer screen and the armaments display while he talked. "We haven't gotten out of the Shenandoah Valley yet, and we've already had two hitters take a stab at us. They were not successful, but we're gettin' a little jumpy out here on this dark old highway. I thought you said this mission was top secret. What gives, sir? Over."

"Carl, I cannot honestly answer your question. This mission is secret. I can count on the fingers of one hand all of the people who are supposed to know what you boys are doing out there. Not even Huntsville knows how we are transporting the product. I'm going to get people on this right now. Now listen to me carefully; until we know more about what is happening here, I want you to proceed as quickly as you possibly can. Don't throw caution to the wind, mind you, but get that contraption to Huntsville by the fastest and safest route. Any questions?"

Marc glanced at Carl. "Give me the mike."

Carl handed the Icom microphone across the console and Marc took it into his left hand. "General, does anybody up there have any idea what is going on here or who might be behind it?" Marc asked.

"Negative, Colonel. You know what I know as of this moment. I'm going to move on the security breach right now. I want to know who could possibly have known you were transporting the device. Until we can dig a little deeper, just keep rolling those wheels. I have a personal call into Agent Crain at the Bureau. If he knows anything or can find out, I'll get back to you. Over."

"Affirmative," Marc said. "We'll keep it on course to Huntsville. If you find anything, you know the number." The squelch tail sounded and Marc waited for a reply.

General Rogers's voice sounded tired and distressed. "Roger, Marc. You guys play it carefully out there. And whatever you do, don't let that device out of your immediate control. Talk to you as soon as I have something more concrete. Over."

"Roger, General," Marc said. "Pathfinder clear." Marc handed the microphone to Carl and focused his attention on the highway. "This isn't making any sense, bro. You got any other ideas?"

"No," Carl said. "I'll feel better when morning comes. I like it better in the daylight when we're out here on the slab. Any hitter with some gumption could park, climb up on a bridge, and wait until we pass and then let the lead fly. Armor or not, it makes me nervous when the shit starts flying."

Marc was lost in thought. He watched the highway become illuminated by the halogen headlights and vanish in white-striped black streaks as the Leeco machine ate blacktop toward Huntsville. "Go into multitasking mode on the computer. Get into NCIC and patch through to motor vehicle registry for Maryland."

Carl punched buttons and keys on the computer keyboard until the patch was completed to Maryland. "Got it. What are you after?"

Marc spoke softly. "A chance to satisfy my curiosity as much as anything. Run Alpha-November-Echo-nine-six-four and see what that comes back registered to."

Marc's mind ran the various possibilities while he recited the numbers.

"What is that?" Carl asked.

"The car that came by us back there. Might be clean, but I'd like to know."

Carl entered the string of numbers and waited while the radio-linked computer accessed and searched the motor vehicle registration files for the state of Maryland. "It's up. Son of a gun, it's a hit."

"What, are you serious?" Marc asked. His voice suddenly perked up and his mind raced now.

"That's what the machine says. Nineteen-eighty-eight Oldsmobile Cutlass stolen from Annapolis on the . . . well, two days ago. What do you think about that?" Carl slapped his hands together and laughed.

"I think things might get interesting. Might have nothing to do with our previous encounters, but then it might be a link. We've got to watch ourselves carefully. My gut tells me we got more company waiting down the slab."

"Yeah," Carl said. "What do you think has happened in Huntsville?"

"Wow, no tellin'. The way this night has gone, nothing I see or hear would surprise me."

The Leeco rig rolled through the Shenandoah Valley south on I-81. Marc checked the speedometer every few seconds to be sure they weren't traveling too fast. He tried to keep the machine near a hundred miles per hour. He watched for traffic and relied heavily upon the Obstacle Detection System and the Collision Avoidance System to keep the rig and users of the highway out of danger. The rig approached the top of a long hill and the halogen headlights shone brightly into the sky beyond the surface of the road. When the rig topped the hill and started down the other side, the CAS blared an alert and the ODS emitted a shrill warning.

"Oh, God!" Marc cried. He gripped the steering wheel and struggled to keep control of the rig while he hit the brakes.

Carl gasped when he looked through the windshield. The highway went through a large cut slope with high embankments on both sides. The perfect ambush setup to stop all traffic on the road. And there, in front of the speeding Leeco rig, the highway was blocked by three tankers and the car that had sped past them earlier.

The Leeco rig screamed rebelliously under the pressure of brakes and sudden deceleration. Marc tried to keep the machine from jackknifing, but more than anything, he tried to keep from colliding with the eighteen-wheelers that blocked the highway.

Jon's patience was growing quite thin. He looked hard at Dr. Caldwell. Everything in his body wanted to kill her and be done with it, but he knew better. If she wasn't bluffing and there was a possibility of a chemical or bacteria spill within the facility, there would be a major problem. And if Dr. Caldwell, uncooperative as she was, was the only one knowledgeable enough to make an accurate determination of such a spill, then he would be foolish to waste such a valuable human resource. Besides that, she was still needed to force her husband into the scheme. Jon knew his people, Ramone especially, were counting on Caldwell's husband's physical resources.

Caldwell was acting like a little puppy dog nipping at its master's heels. She wouldn't let go and she wouldn't quit. "You really are scared, aren't you, Jon?"

Jon put on his meanest face and shot back at

Caldwell, "You had best let it ride, Dr. Caldwell, before I yield to my better judgment and handle you like I have handled the others in the back of this facility. Put bluntly, my dear lady . . . don't push it."

Caldwell shot back an indignant face and turned her head.

"Dennis!" Jon bellowed.

"Yes, sir?" Dennis answered. He stepped back into the doorway and faced Jon.

"Get two of our technical types and check the elevator for function. If there is difficulty, I want to know about it as soon as practical. If it requires repair, I want an assessment of the time frame and materials needed."

"Yes, sir," Dennis said. He turned immediately and disappeared down the hallway.

"Now, Dr. Bad Attitude, let's you and me take a stroll through this institution of death. No nonsense from you. I want to see all of these research rooms and the storage rooms. Play games with me and I will terminate you. Do I make myself clear?"

Dr. Caldwell stood erect. "If you look very closely, you can see me tremble."

"Dr. Caldwell," von Wirth said. "Please try to cooperate with Jon. He is a man dedicated to his mission. It will only worsen the outcome if we do not cooperate with him in every way we can."

"I don't believe you, Dr. von Wirth. You are involved with these people. How?" Dr. Caldwell was demanding and arrogant and she made no effort to hide her disapproval.

"Dr. Caldwell, there is so much about this operation that you do not know and would not understand if you did. Let me sum it up very briefly. Our funding from the American government was discontinued ten years ago. A special arrangement with a senator and a businessman from your state of Kentucky has managed to keep this operation both functional and secret. We have worked on many projects in this underground hole. To the American people, this place was closed years ago. Only a handful of individuals in the government even knows it ever existed, much less knows of its continuing operation. This man is here to liberate us to a place where we may continue our work without government interference or fear of discovery. I see you do not like him very much. That is your prerogative. But please, doctor, you are a brilliant scientist and a great mind. Treat this man with at least a little respect."

Dr. Caldwell's face took on a puzzled look. "You mean to tell me we haven't been working for the government all these years?"

"Yes and no. Perhaps when this is concluded satisfactorily, I shall explain the nature of our work here. We manufacture the formulas for death. You already know that. What we have all learned to accept and understand is that sometimes it is necessary to have and maintain and ensure life. Does that make sense to you, Dr. Caldwell?"

"We are caught on the brink of madness here, aren't we, Dr. von Wirth? And you, sir, are a player in a game of total insanity. You know as well as I that it would be virtual genocide to move some of these compounds and viruses to the outside world. We have in this facility a stable, controlled environment where we can monitor, study, and understand the nature of these organisms and chemical mixtures. To unleash them on the outside world for anything less than a last-ditch effort to save this country or mankind in general would be an unforgivable sin. Do you want that on your conscience?"

Jon wasn't sure what he was hearing. He looked at

von Wirth. "Dr. von Wirth, would you again please translate what this person just said."

Von Wirth ran his wrinkled fingers through his white hair once more. He took a deep breath and looked Jon squarely in the eyes. "Jon, she is saying that if these compounds, and particularly these bacterial organisms, ever made their way into the atmosphere of the earth . . . well, there might not be anyone left to inhabit this planet. What we deal with in this unit is potent and it is very, very deadly. And Dr. Caldwell is right when she says that even we do not know the full ramifications of our work. If there has been a spill because of the tremor, none of us will ever have the opportunity to know. I'm afraid Dr. Caldwell's descriptions of the manifestations of some of our organisms is quite accurate. Perhaps it would be beneficial to all concerned if we have more cooperation and less hostility. None of us are in a position to stop the others without causing harm to us all . . . to all of the human race."

Dennis stepped back inside the door to von Wirth's private sector. "Jon, we have an analysis."

"So why do you keep me in suspense?" Jon asked angrily.

"There is damage, but our techs think they can repair it without extensive materials. Looks like an electrical problem."

"And the estimated time of repair is?" Jon asked.

"One, maybe two hours, depending on the full extent of the damage," Dennis said confidently.

"It must be done in half of that. I want those eighteen-wheel trucks rolling on the highway before dawn. I cannot, this mission will not, tolerate any delays. Do I make myself clear?"

Dennis stepped back until he was directly in the

middle of the doorway. He looked into the area outside of von Wirth's office and then he looked back at Jon. "Yes, sir, but I'm only the messenger, not the repairman. I'll relay the word. I'm sure those men want out of here just as badly as you and I, sir."

"Tell them to get about the business of making repairs. I want results and not excuses. We have to load all of those trucks before dawn. The men in the mission control will be ready to leave this place and we will be entrapped in some antiseptic mole hole. I will not tolerate it."

"Yes, sir," Dennis said, and he was out of the door and into the entrance area near the elevator before Jon could address him again.

Jon faced Dr. Caldwell. "Now, doctor, it is time for you and me to make the inspection you indicated." He gestured toward the door. "Shall we?"

Dr. Caldwell hesitated, fire in her eyes, but she thought better of it and walked through the door. "Have you ordered all of the others in the residences killed?"

"Most, but not all. Why?"

"I'll tell you why. These people were my companions . . . my friends. Killing them is unnecessary."

"I am not a man subject to excessive compassion, Dr. Caldwell. I am a man who believes in missions. That is all I am concerned about. Where I come from, lives are expendable. They represent merely the tally for accomplishing a mission. And in all operations of a strategic nature, there are root numbers that represent acceptable losses. Men are merely tools to accomplish work. Those who have no value are cast aside."

Dr. Caldwell led the way down the hallway through a maze of security locks and doorways. "You know what you have done here is murder, don't you?"

Jon laughed. "Such an attitude. How is that you and I differ in our work? I kill people for money. You kill people for money. Our work—yours as well as mine—represents death. The underlying difference is that I have the fortitude to look into the eyes of those I kill. You send your death by invisible means on the wind or on the nose of an intercontinental ballistic missile. You don't have to look at the ones you kill. I wonder if you had to see your victims, if you would continue your work. Would you, Dr. Caldwell?"

Dr. Caldwell stopped, turned, and spat fire from her eyes as she looked at Jon. "What I do, I do in the name of science, for the benefit of all mankind. I am a scientist, a researcher."

"Labels." Jon laughed and shook his head. "You Americans have such a way with labels. You think your definitions will negate the effect or intent of your actions. Do you ever wonder why so many people from so many countries hate you?"

Dr. Caldwell moved both hands to her chest and grabbed the ends of her nightgown. She tugged hard and pulled them together. "You are in our country . . . *my* country. You do not belong here. You came here with criminal intent. You have killed Americans and now you have the balls to look me in the face and ask me why people hate Americans? Perhaps you would do better to ask yourself why Americans hate people from other countries."

Jon shot her a dirty look, but he made no further comment.

Caldwell turned around and walked several feet to a monitor console filled with electrical and scientific instruments. She scanned them and peered through the thick glass windows into one of the laboratories. "The instruments read okay for this room. I would feel better if I made a visual inspection before we move to the next one. We took quite a jolt from that tremor. Something could have jarred loose."

Jon gestured toward the door, but said nothing.

"We need to suit up just in case."

"In case of what? What suit?"

"An environmental suit. Surely you have seen television photographs of our astronauts. We use a suit similar in appearance and function to work around these chemicals and organisms. How do you think we keep them from killing us?"

"And just where are these suits?" Jon asked.

"In that room," Dr. Caldwell said. She pointed to a room marked DECONTAMINATION UNIT #1. The room was across the narrow hallway to their left. It looked more like a closet door than the entry to a functional room.

"How many suits are in this room?"

"Six."

"And that is all you have in this facility?"

"No. We have a decontam room for each lab. There are fifteen labs and fifteen rooms. We also have a master decontam room where we routinely inspect and repair suits. You must remember, this laboratory is virtually self-sufficient with the exception of certain fuels and chemicals that we must replenish periodically."

Jon said, "I care nothing of that. I want to get these materials on those trucks up on the surface. That is what I care about."

"You'd better care if you want to stay alive down here," Caldwell said.

"What does that mean?" Jon asked harshly.

"It means that the red indicator light that just started flashing on the bottom panel of this console indicates a slight rupture of one of the bacterial holding canisters in lab one. We have a leak, and if it isn't contained, you won't have to worry about that elevator not working, because none of us will be leaving this unit alive. And that, Jon, includes you . . . mission or no mission."

# Chapter Nine

□ □ □

Dermont Ashland felt completely helpless. He looked at the men with the guns pointed at him, then at Frank. When their eyes met, they both looked to the floor at the body of Ramone sprawled lifelessly in front of them.

Slowly and deliberately, both Ashland and Frank lifted their hands over their heads and interlaced their fingers just like the big man with the automatic pointed at them had ordered.

"Very good," the agent said. "I am Special Agent Mitch Lovell. I am going to issue you a series of commands. If you do not immediately obey those commands or if you refuse, these men and I will use whatever force is necessary to ensure your compliance with those commands even if it means deadly force. Do you understand me?"

Ashland and Frank nodded to indicate they understood Agent Lovell.

"Good, then we're off to a fine start. Now, Dermont Ashland, I want you to kneel to the floor while keeping your hands over your head. Do it now!"

Ashland complied.

"Now, Frank Montino, you do exactly what Ashland did. Do it now."

Frank hesitated, but then complied as well.

"Good. Ashland . . . cross your legs behind your back."

Ashland did as he was told.

"Good. Montino, the same thing. Do it now!"

Frank obeyed the command.

"Now, both of you together. Stretch your hands as far in front of you as you can. Keep the fingers interlaced. When you have done that, lean forward until your hands touch the floor as far from your body as you can reach. This one's tricky. You mess up and we will respond accordingly. Do you understand?"

Frank and Ashland nodded. They kept their eyes forward and leaned with their hands extended in front of them until they lost balance and their body weight shifted to their hands that now rested upon the floor.

"Very good. Now, lay on the floor while keeping your hands far out in front of you. Montino, don't even consider going for that weapon. These are ten-millimeter Smith and Wessons. They make a very nasty hole when they tear through flesh."

Frank looked at the agent, but he said nothing.

"Do you understand my command?" Lovell asked.

Once more, Ashland and Frank nodded yes.

"Do it now!"

Frank made it to the floor before Ashland. He leaned with all of his weight on his arms, then he slid them forward and lay down.

"Good," Lovell said. He kept the barrel of the Model 1006 Smith & Wesson aimed at Frank's head. "Now, Montino . . . spread your hands in a spread-eagle position until they rest firmly on the floor with the palms up. Do you understand me?"

Frank nodded yes and obeyed the command.

"Now, Ashland, you do the same. Any questions?"

Ashland nodded no and proceeded to do just as Frank had done.

"Very good. Do it nice and slowly," Lovell said.

Ashland was halfway to the floor from the kneeling position when he dropped suddenly. He gasped for breath and his body trembled. He clawed at the carpet with the tips of his fingers, then moved his hands back over his chest in an instinctive move.

Lovell barked, "Ashland, hands in front of you. Now! Ashland."

Frank turned his head toward Ashland, then back at Lovell. "He's having a heart attack. He needs help. I swear, he's in respiratory distress. He needs an ambulance."

Lovell was unyielding. He kept the barrel of the 1006 aimed at Ashland. "Norman, check Ashland. Montino . . . don't move unless I order you to move. Understood?"

Frank looked at Ashland again. "Yes, dammit, I understand. I understand this man needs an ambulance and you are denying him medical treatment."

"Quiet, Montino. How is he, Norman?"

Agent Norman leaned over Ashland from the rear. He touched his skin and then his carotid artery for a pulse. "Skin is cool and clammy. Pulse is weak and irregular. He's in respiratory distress. I think it's real, sir. We'd better get an ambulance."

"Damn," Lovell said. "Okay, cuff Montino and move back. Carlisle, get on the horn and get an ambulance over here. Tell them what we've got and have them come to the back of the house. That seems to be the most popular entry tonight."

Agent Carlisle obeyed without hesitation. In less than a second, he was out of the room.

Agent Lovell stood with his weapon still at arm's length and trained on Montino.

Agent Norman did a quick pat-down on Montino and reached for the .45 automatic tucked inside his waistband.

Norman's move gave Montino the opportunity he had waited for. He moved fast, his legs flying upward and into Norman's crotch. He kicked once very hard and then kicked again before Norman could react. Then Montino rolled left, grabbed Norman, and threw him in the line of fire between himself and the other agents.

Gunfire roared.

Lovell fired first. His reaction to pull his shot was too late.

The first .40-caliber rounds struck Norman in the face and chest. The agent slammed backward, but Montino was already rolling to cover and firing position. He cleared his waistband with the .45 automatic and thumbed the hammer back. He fired fast and accurately. Two 230-grain hardballers punched cylindrical holes through Lovell's face. His head jackhammered back and he disappeared from sight.

Two more agents opened fire. Their shots flew wild and missed Montino. He rolled again and fired a pair of double-taps. The shots tagged each of the agents in the neck and upper chest. Blood flew across the room in a splotchy mist from severed carotid arteries. Both agents fell dead to the floor.

Four down, two to go.

Frank rolled up and made it to his feet. He went after the agent who had ducked out of the door when the shooting started. He hit the doorway and fell into a crouch. He rolled into the foyer, the muzzle of his auto searching for a target.

It found none.

He swiveled to his feet again. He swept the area in front of him and to his sides with the muzzle of the .45 automatic. He worked his way rapidly through the house toward the back, where he guessed the agents had made entry. He went to the outside door and looked. He saw no one, but he did see their cars. They were parked in the long driveway beside the house that was lit with a dozen lamps on wrought-iron posts.

Frank moved out of the door and slipped into the shadow of shrubbery that lined the back wall of the house. He moved slowly and carefully, his senses alert and his honed killing skills sharpened to a razor's edge.

He heard the engine start on one of the cars. Then he saw them. Both agents in one car and they were on the run.

Montino made a tactical magazine change and slipped another stick of hardball into the well of the Colt. He dropped the other partially fired magazine into his pocket and made a maddening run for the car.

The agents spotted him. One of them, the passenger, leaned out of the window and opened fire.

The shots missed. Montino dropped to his knees. He took point-shoulder aim and fired. He dumped the new stick into the car, alternating from the driver's to the passenger's side. Eight shots were fired and the slide locked back.

The engine gunned on the car, but it was out of gear.

Montino ran toward the car and crammed another stick into the Colt. He flipped the slide release and let it rake the top round from the magazine. The Colt slammed into battery with the hammer back and ready to fire.

He reached the car and looked in over the sights of the Colt. Both agents were dead, the interior of the car splattered in dark red blood. He reached in on the driver's side and shut off the engine. He tossed the keys into the shrubbery and ran back toward the house.

When he got inside, Ashland was almost blue. His breathing was very shallow and his skin felt moist and clammy. He knelt down and lifted the old man by his shoulders. He slung him, struggling all the while, over his own shoulders and stumbled from the house.

Once outside, he found one of the FBI cars with the keys still in it. He opened the rear door on the dark sedan and gently laid Dermont Ashland into the backseat. He slammed the door closed and hopped into the driver's seat. He hit the ignition and fired the engine. When the fed car hit the main road in front of Dermont Ashland's house, Frank turned right and headed for Ashland Transportation Services. He knew the last place the feds would look would be in an overroad eighteen-wheeler headed south.

When the rumbling and the explosions stopped, Sikes couldn't believe he was still alive. He wasn't really sure he was. He moved his legs first, then his arms. To his amazement, they both worked. He managed to force himself from the floor and to his knees. Outside the guard shack, there was a gaping hole where the floor had been only seconds or minutes before. Sikes wasn't sure how long it had been, because he wasn't sure if he had been knocked unconscious or if his temporary loss of memory was caused by the punishing concussion from the series of explosions.

He looked at Peterson, who had come to cover his back side. There were pools of blood beneath him on what remained of the floor. The guy's clothing was shredded and there were streaks of blood trickling down his opened flesh. One look at Peterson's face, and Sikes knew he was dead.

His assault rifle lay on the floor behind him. Sikes reached over and picked it up. He checked to be sure everything was functional.

It was.

He managed to stand now, his legs weak and rubbery. He scanned his work in the video switching controller. With the control center a smoking, burning heap of rubble, there would be no need for the video unit now. He found his field pack and slung it over his shoulders. That's when he realized just how badly he hurt. Pain tortured his body, but he found no open wounds and no sign of blood trickling from his ears, so he diagnosed himself whole and uninjured.

Outside, through the area where the double glass doors had been before, Sikes could hear sirens wailing in the distance. He made a quick assumption that they were headed for the control center. That meant he had to get out of the building and out of the area as quickly as possible.

Smoke thickened and made breathing difficult, if not almost impossible. The smell was rancid, putrid, and acidic all mixed together. It reminded him of a burned transformer in a piece of electronic gear, but it was magnified a million times, as if thousands of transformers had smoked at once in a small confined area.

Sikes assessed the situation outside of the guard shack. There was little floor remaining, and the holes that occupied the space once sealed by steel and concrete now acted as escape routes for towers of smoke and tongues of flame.

There was only one way out. He would have to hug the walls and hope the floor supports didn't give way beneath his weight. But with the smoke growing worse by the second, there was no time to deliberate.

He moved over the body in the doorway and out onto the jagged edge of the floor. He leaned heavily against the wall of the guard shack and worked his way along it until he could see the opening to the outside. He couldn't see or hear anything except the sound of the sirens coming closer from somewhere beyond the control center.

Seconds passed like hours until he reached the doorway to the outside. The glass had been shattered into shards and slivers that littered the sidewalk leading to the roadway. He saw the eighteen-wheeler; it appeared to have retained its integrity despite the explosions. He moved toward it.

That's when he heard somebody call his name.

Sikes jerked around shakily, his assault rifle coming on line in the direction of the voice. His finger eased the trigger back until he could feel the sear ready to slip. Then he paused and held his finger as steady as he could. He could see the figure who had called out his name now.

Roger Spiker.

Spiker walked toward Sikes, his own assault rifle ready to spit fire and death. When he reached Sikes, he let the muzzle drop toward the ground. "We got to get away from here. It's all gone nuts now. Everybody inside must be dead. How did you get out?"

"I'm not sure," Sikes said. "I came to and I was lying on the floor. Peterson caught a load of shrapnel and took the hit. I guess he saved my life after all. Do you know what happened?"

"No, I just know the whole damned world erupted. I was outside on the other side of the building when it

came. I had taken the guard's body to the chem tanker.
I can't believe this."

Sirens grew louder now, and through the dense
smoke that billowed out of the mission control center,
both men could see flashing red lights coming toward
them.

"Let's book," Spiker said. "Looks like it's just you
and me."

The men ran as hard as they could toward the
chemical tanker parked a quarter of a mile away near the
entrance to the underground facility. Both were weary
and shaky. Their efforts to run were more reflexive than
intentional. They staggered and fell twice, but they
knew there was no time to stop and further assess the
situation.

They stumbled and moved through every available
cover until they had the tanker in sight. Both were
struggling for breath and still suffering from the effects of
the concussion caused by the blast.

They reached the overroad tanker.

"We've got to get out of this compound before
everything is sealed off by internal security. If we hang
around long, they're going to nail us," Spiker said.

"What about the mission?" Sikes asked.

"To hell with the mission. This is survival now. Let
the old man in Kentucky worry about the damned
mission. I told him not to hire those foreign screwballs,
but he wouldn't listen. I told him and Frank tried to tell
him. Now maybe if somebody doesn't ice his ass, he'll
know what we were talking about."

Sikes tried to catch his breath. He was still very
unsteady on his feet. His breathing came hard and his
lungs hurt from the inhalation of too much smoke. "Do
you know what happened down in the control room?"

"No; like I said, I was outside. If I hadn't been, I

wouldn't be here. They were in the critical stages of wiring the radio-activated explosives in place when I left to come up to you. Like the intelligence said, one wire out of place and . . . *bang*. Well, it went bang. That's all I know."

Sikes leaned against the tractor of the chemical truck. He bent over and let his outstretched arms rest on his knees. "If we're the only ones who got out, what are we going to do now?"

"We need to change out of these clothes and get this rig rolling. I figure it's our best shot at getting out of this place without too much hassle or a firefight. These people are gonna be on their toes and watching every-thing that moves. Hell, what time is it? My watch got crunched in the blast."

Sikes looked at his watch. "Zero-three-fifty."

"Yeah, it'll be daylight in a little over an hour. We got to get out of here. Where are your clothes?"

"In the other rig," Sikes said.

"Mine too," Spiker said. "Let's get them and get a move on before someone sees us."

"I'm surprised there are so few people here at night. You'd think security would be tighter. Guess it's lucky for us it's not, huh?"

"Later," Spiker said. "We can chitchat once we get this rig out of the compound and on the open road. I'll breathe easier when that machine is chewing white lines on I-65 south."

Both men ran toward the second eighteen-wheeler parked twenty yards from the tanker. They reached it, manipulated the locks on the trailer door, and climbed inside. They rummaged through backpacks until they found their clothing. Sikes watched the door and the area around them while Spiker stripped from his field utilities and dressed again in jeans, boots, and a flannel shirt. When Spiker was finished, he covered the door so Sikes could change.

"That's it," Sikes said. "Now I feel better. I'm a trucker, not a damned commando."

When Sikes got to the door of the trailer, he could see the first firefighting units arriving on the scene. Red lights flashed everywhere and men in long waterproof coats pulled and tugged on hoses. Security personnel were also moving around in total disarray. He looked at Spiker, who watched nervously while the responding personnel frantically tried to start water pumping onto the flaming ruins of the control center.

"Let's do it," Spiker said. "Whatever happens, stay calm. We just got caught in here with a load of chemicals and we're afraid they're going to blow if they get too hot. That's the line. You got it?"

"What about the people down below in the lab? Do we just leave them?"

"Hey, man, that's their problem," Spiker said. "This thing is all out of whack now and nothing is gonna put it back on track again. Let 'em make their own way. I'm covering my ass and gettin' the hell out of here."

"I'm with you," Sikes said. "We still got people on the gate. What do we do when we get there?"

"We'll make that decision when we get there. Move out."

Sikes and Spiker hit the ground on the run. They ran to the tanker and Spiker climbed into the cab on the driver's side. Sikes took the passenger door.

Spiker fired the diesel engine, let it warm a few seconds, then dropped the big machine into gear. The rig spat and coughed because it hadn't had enough time to warm, but it slowly moved forward. Spiker turned it around and headed out of the compound. He drove

slowly when he approached the only roadway out . . .
the one that went past the burning control center.

Spiker eased the rig past fire trucks, ambulances,
and security personnel, all of whom appeared to be
frantically working to extinguish the flaming, smoking
center.

They were almost at the turn past the building
when a security man armed with a shotgun stepped into
the roadway. He held up a orange-coned flashlight to
indicate he wanted the truck to stop.

"Oh, shit," Sikes said.

"Be cool, man. Let me handle him," Spiker replied.
He eased the rig to the point where the security man
stood with the light. He rolled the window down and
hung his left elbow out. "Howdy, what the hell happened over there?" Spiker asked the guard.

"What are you doing in here at this hour of the
morning?" the guard asked.

"Makin' our usual delivery," Spiker said.

"I'll need some identification and your transportation papers. This area is sealed off because of the fire and
explosions. Nothing other than firefighting equipment
and emergency-service personnel are permitted in or
out. I'm afraid you won't be able to leave for a while."

"I respect that," Spiker said, "but I got over two
thousand gallons of high-test potent chemicals in that
tank back there. If this baby gets the wrong spark or gets
too hot, it's gonna go like a Roman candle on the Fourth
of July. You ain't seen a bang until you see some of this
crap blow. It's highly volatile, highly toxic, and the
fumes alone could kill people from here to Ardmore. I've
got to get this thing away from this compound before she
gets fidgety and decides to blow."

The guard was unsympathetic. He swung the shotgun toward Spiker and his face hardened. "I will not

permit you to leave this compound. Open the door slowly and step from the cab." The guard stepped back so he could see further into the cab. "Passenger, you do the same thing. Slide across the seat and exit on the driver's side. I will use this shotgun if you do not do exactly what I tell you."

Spiker hesitated. His right hand left the steering wheel and slid the Ruger P-85 9mm automatic from his waistband. He moved slowly to open the door once the Ruger was trained on the position where the guard was standing.

"Now!" the guard yelled.

"Okay, all ready," Spiker said. He swung the door open and fired the Ruger in the same motion. He fired again and again until the guard fell to the pavement.

Spiker slammed the door closed and kicked the rig back into gear, let the clutch out, and floored the accelerator.

A shot rang out, then another. The guard was down and firing his shotgun. The first load of double-O buckshot caught Spiker in the side of the head. The second load missed the cab and slammed into the body of the 306 tanker. The hot lead balls penetrated the stainless-steel outer shell, riveted through the cork liner, and exited into the tank through the aluminum inner body of the tanker.

Chemicals trickled from holes and seeped to the ground. The rig stopped, the engine choked down when Spiker's dead foot left the accelerator.

A third shot echoed and more security men came running from half a block back. This time, more holes appeared and the tanker leaked profusely.

Sikes jumped from the rig before it stopped. He hit the ground running, his assault rifle firing hot lead toward the rushing guards. One went down and a third dropped to his knees. More gunfire rang out into the dark Huntsville night. Sikes felt the searing, burning pain when sizzling pellets chewed through his flesh and slammed into several vital organs. He plummeted to the ground, his assault rifle firing desperation hellfire toward the guards as he died. But the last death rounds missed the rushing men and slammed into the body of the 306 stainless-sheathed tanker. And as Sikes rolled on the ground in his death throes, he saw the fires of hell erupt behind him. The night became bright with an orange fireball; flaming death reached into the darkness and consumed him.

# Chapter Ten

□ □ □

There was no way to stop and nowhere to go except into the rigs that blocked the interstate highway.

Marc fought frantically for control of the rig. It skidded, swerved, and fishtailed, but still wouldn't stop.

Carl was stunned. The impending collision approached in hazy slow motion. He took his eyes off the rigs ahead and focused on the computer screen. He pressed the key for multitasking mode and switched to armaments without even thinking. Instinct took control of his actions; his mind was in full survival mode. He found the screen and pressed the instant pod retractors. Then he took a chance and pressed the firing mechanism on the LAR rockets without waiting for the pod-lock indicator prompt on the screen. Loud whooshes rocked the Leeco machine and clouds of streaming white smoke shot ahead of the rig in spiraling trails that were etched with fire.

The highway ahead, less than two hundred yards now, erupted blinding orange with a cataclysmic explosion that made the ground beneath the Leeco rig tremble. The giant oval-shaped gasoline tankers that blocked the highway disappeared in a fireball lined with thick, black smoke. The smoke churned into the night sky in roaring funnels that twisted and spiraled into the darkness above the fire.

The Leeco rig was closing in on the holocaust now. Less than a hundred yards remained between the rig and the flaming ruins of the tankers and the bandit car.

"Hold tight," Marc yelled.

The giant custom overroad rig smashed into the inferno at over fifty miles per hour. The collision rocked the Leeco machine and tossed Marc and Carl forward and then sideways inside the cab. They fought for balance, but Marc still held tightly to the steering wheel.

The roadblock wedge opened up and sent fiery debris raining in every direction along the Virginia landscape when the Highway Warriors penetrated the other side. Fiery residue shrouded the Leeco machine and enveloped it in a halo of reddish orange for a few seconds, then extinguished itself in the slipstream as Marc accelerated.

When the rig was a half mile down the road, Marc slowed to a stop. "Think we should go back?" he asked.

"I don't know. You think anybody lived through that?"

"Could be. Let's go take a look."

"How do you propose we do that? There are no median crossovers in sight," Carl said.

"Let's just turn around and go back. I don't imagine any traffic will be coming through that mess."

Carl looked hard at Marc, puzzled. "You want to turn this rig around and go the wrong way on the superslab." Carl shook his head. "Man, I worry about you sometimes, but hell, you're the driver."

Marc proceeded to turn the rig around in the middle of the interstate highway. He moved from shoulder to shoulder until he had the machine headed back toward the fiery mess in the highway. "You saved our lives back there. That was good, quick thinking. It makes me glad you're my partner."

"Yeah, thanks. You didn't do so badly yourself. You could have lost the machine and just crashed into the inferno. You aimed real well at the wedge."

Marc watched the highway ahead. Traffic on the other side of the interstate was light to nonexistent, which helped. He rolled the rig near the burning, twisted metal and stopped. There was no sign of life anywhere.

"What do you think?" Carl asked. "Dead or running?"

"My guess is some of both." Marc reached behind the seat and grabbed his silenced Uzi and musette bag. "Let's go carefully and slowly. When we get out, I'll take the left, you take the right. If you encounter resistance, try to keep one alive. I'd like to get some answers."

"Take the Icoms and the tac headsets?"

"Affirmative. Stay on channel thirteen."

"Affirmative," Carl said. He reached behind his seat and removed the carrying cases for the Icom U-16 transceivers. He handed one to Marc and slipped the other on his belt with the metal belt clip.

Marc took the radio and also slipped it on his belt. He adjusted the wire harness to the throat microphone around his back and then strapped the mike and earphone in place. He switched on the voice-operated switch attached to the microphone harness and spoke. "Am I on?"

"You got it," Carl replied. He also finished installing the VOX harness on his radio and tested it to be sure everything was functioning correctly. When he was done, he looked at Marc and nodded.

"Let's do it," Marc said. He opened the door on the rig and climbed from the cab. On the other side of the wreckage, traffic was slowly snarling. Drivers looked out of their cars at the inferno, but no one came forward.

Carl slid from the passenger's seat and climbed from his side of the cab. He swept the firelit night with the muzzle of his Uzi. He searched for a target, but nothing moved.

"Use a wide arcing sweep to go in. I don't see anything on this side," Marc said. His voice was projected through the throat microphone and transmitted through the Icom U-16 while his hands rested on the Uzi.

"Roger," Carl said. "I don't see anything moving over here either."

"Okay, let's close and see what pops up."

"Roger. It's pretty warm on this side. I hope the explosions are history," Carl replied.

The words had hardly cleared his throat when the first shots came from the darkness at the top of the cut slope. Carl spun around and looked for the source of the gunfire.

He couldn't see it.

More shots came. Carl ran to the other side of the Leeco rig near where he had last seen Marc. "You see the shooter?" he asked into the tac harness.

"Negative," Marc replied. He crouched down at the back end of the Leeco trailer opposite where the gunfire had come from and scanned the dark top of the cut slope for a sign of the shooter. He saw nothing but darkness and embers from burning debris that drifted lazily back to earth from the charred wreckage.

"I'll try to spot his muzzle flash when he taps off another burst. When I peg him, you make a wide approach from the rear. I'll lay enough cover fire to get attention off of you. Is that a roger?"

"Roger," Marc replied. He kept his eyes on the top

of the slope, occasionally taking a quick glance across the broad face of the weed-lined hillside.

Carl stayed low, but the heat from the burning wreckage intensified as he hid behind the cover of the Leeco rig. Then the gunfire came again.

There were two shooters this time. Muzzle flashes came from two different locations at the top of the slope simultaneously.

Carl pointed the muzzle of the Uzi in the direction of the top and fired into the darkness. The Uzi sputtered with the fusillade of sizzling death pellets. The shooters held their fire and waited.

Marc raced from the rear of the rig. He kept low and ran a zigzag pattern to make his profile more difficult for the hitters at the top of the hill to aim at. "Hey, bro. See if you can get into the rig on the driver's side. Get inside and activate the infrared scanners on the electronic sight. Track them on top and get a head count."

"Affirmative," Carl replied. "Watch your ass until I'm in place."

"You can count on it," Marc replied. He made his way through the ditch that bordered the roadway. He stayed as close to the slope as he possibly could to take advantage of any cover it might afford him. He moved seventy-five yards south, behind the rig, and then started up the embankment. He made his way slowly, scouring the top of the hill as he moved.

Then he saw a flash. It wasn't a muzzle flash this time, but a reflection off of the barrel of a weapon illuminated by the intensely burning overroad rigs on the highway. He dropped to a crouch and took careful aim. The object disappeared. Marc dropped the barrel of the Uzi and decided the shot was too far anyway. He stood to a crouch again and moved up the hill in the direction of the flash. He worked his way slowly, checking his footing and the terrain in front of him before he took each step up the steep hillside. Over the crackle of the fire on the highway, Marc heard the sound of an approaching siren. And if that siren was a police car, he knew there would be more trouble than he could explain his way out of in a reasonable period of time.

"I'm in and scanning the top, bro," Carl said into the microphone.

"Roger," Marc replied. "We got more problems. I hear a siren coming. Can't tell if it's a cop or a fire unit. Either way, I'd just as soon not be here when they arrive. What do you think?"

"There are people up there. I see five images on the screen. Might be more over the crest of the slope on the back side. I'm like you, I'd just as soon not be here when the authorities come. I'd like to have a face-to-face chat with those assholes on top, though."

"Too late to run now," Marc said. "Blue lights topping the crest of the hill. We got company."

"Roger," Carl replied. "I see the light through the fire. What now?"

"We wing it and wait for the officers' reaction to this mess. I'm going to move up on top and see if I can get a handle on where these guys are holding up. Can you keep them on the infrared?"

"Affirmative. I'll keep 'em on as long as they stay on this side of the hill."

"Looks like a state trooper. He's out of his car and walking toward the wreckage. Sit tight. I can watch everything he does from up here. If he comes too close, I'll warn you."

"Affirmative."

A long burst of automatic-weapons fire erupted from the top of the hill. The fire was directed toward the trooper this time. Marc watched helplessly as the outgunned and outnumbered officer of the law sought cover.

The trooper drew his weapon and returned fire in the direction from which it had come. He stayed below the front fender of his patrol car and waited to see if fire was returned from the hillside.

Another burst opened up from the top. The trooper rose up over the fender and fired a single shot from his revolver. He ducked down as quickly as he had risen up.

The trooper tried to get into the passenger's side of his patrol car, but the door was locked. He did a duck walk from the fender to the door and then back again.

Another sporadic burst of gunfire came from the hill. The windshield on the police vehicle cracked from the impact of hostile projectiles. Shards of glass flew and the trooper covered his face and head from the flying shrapnel. When the barrage stopped, the trooper raised the barrel of his weapon over the lip of the fender and fired two shots.

More auto fire came from the hill. Three shooters at once fired on the officer. The trooper stayed low and tried to shield himself from the savage hellstorm.

"Give him a hand," Marc said over the radio. "They've got him pinned down beside his car. Send some sizzling hornets from the Stingers into the hill and see if that makes any attitude adjustment."

Carl lined the electronic infrared sight on the last shooter he had seen spitting hellfire from a bore. He settled the circular X on the man's image and touched the firing mechanism for a second.

A roar of thunder belched from the rotary guns of the Stinger assembly. A stream of angry hornets spat from the barrels and found the flesh of the man who was imaged on the screen. The 5.56mm death missiles chewed through the man and perforated his body like a sieve before he ever knew what hit him.

The gunfire from that point on the hill stopped and Carl saw the image fall prone.

"Zippered that one," Carl said. "I'm gonna give one of the others a thrill. Watch this." He pressed the keys to set the electronic sight on automatic imaging. He touched his finger to the firing mechanism and another spray of death pelted into the hilltop.

"Nailed him," Marc said. He heard the death scream of the man. Tiny tumblers punched holes through the shooter's dying body. "Watch the trooper. He's moving."

More gunfire came from the hill. The trooper made a foolish move and ran for the driver's side of his car. A fast burst of automatic fire punched life from him before he could get to his destination.

"Trooper is down. Repeat, trooper is down. Let the others you can see on the sight have a taste of hellfire à la mode."

Carl touched the firing mechanism and held it for a second or more. Another roar thundered through the Leeco rig. The Stinger directed a bullet every two square inches in an area the size of a large conference table. The death messengers found their target and left another shooter in a pile of shredded flesh and blood-splattered bone.

"Good shooting, Major," Marc said. "Keep that hot number off of me. I'm moving now. I want to try to take the one on the end nearest me without having to kill him. If he moves, keep him tracked on the imager."

"Roger," Carl replied. "I got his number on the screen. If he gets too brave, I'll change his attitude permanently and send him into everlasting peace."

Marc moved out cautiously. He worked his way to

the top of the slope, checked out the back side, and then moved ten or twelve feet from the crest down the back side. He moved four or five feet at a time then stopped to look and listen for movement from the shooters.

He saw none.

Carl's voice crackled through the earpiece on Marc's Icom. "I still have three images on the screen, bro. I'm tracking and holding steady on all of 'em. Where are you?"

Marc whispered softly so he wouldn't reveal his position. "I'm on the back side and moving just below the crest. It's dark as pitch up here. All I can see is the glow from the fire down there. If these guys move, they'll be perfectly silhouetted against the fire. Keep me posted on any movement."

"You'll be the first to know," Carl replied.

"I'll be on radio silence for the next few minutes. If you have traffic, just give it and don't worry if I don't answer. I'm moving in on the guy at the end."

"Affirmative. One more thing—be careful."

"Always," Marc replied. He moved toward the end shooter who lay low in the weeds at the crest of the cut slope. Sound generated from movement wasn't much of a problem because of the noise from the crackling fire on the highway. And the collective noise generated by cars stopping behind the wreckage offered further protection for his assault.

Marc moved close to the ground almost in a duck walk. He could see the outline of the guy he wanted. The man appeared as a large, dark blob lying on the ground in the weeds. Marc fixed his eyes slightly to the right of the man, not taking any chances that some sixth sense would trigger an alert in the guy's mind and cause him to turn around. He moved forward slowly, the silenced Uzi steady in his hands and ready to spit eternal hellfire if it came to that.

The man moved. He shifted his weight and straightened his legs. Then he twisted his head and looked behind him. He apparently didn't see anything that concerned him, so he turned back around and faced the highway.

Marc went down in the weeds and stayed perfectly still. He kept his eyes fixed on the shooter. And now he could see it . . . an M-16 assault rifle. The shooter had it fixed on his left arm and his right hand wrapped around the pistol grip. The guy watched every movement on the roadway.

When the shooter appeared settled, Marc moved. He slipped closer to his target . . . fifteen feet to go now.

Marc crept slowly and stealthily. His surgically sharp combat senses were fully alert. Ten feet to go.

The shooter was unaware of his presence.

Then a voice from somewhere to the right of the stalked shooter rang out into the night. "Open up on that damned truck."

Gunfire livened the night. Assault-rifle fire licked from hot barrels as tongues of flame sent hellfire toward the Leeco rig.

Marc dropped prone and lifted the Uzi on line with the shooter he could see. The man's M-16 chattered and hot brass pelted the ground beside him. The pungent smell of burned gunpowder drifted across the humid night air and displaced the smell of burning petroleum from the highway.

Marc took a chance. He came to his feet and moved hard and fast. He closed the distance to the shooter and jumped on top of the guy like he was mounting a bronco.

The shooter tried to roll over and his assault rifle fell silent. Marc crammed the barrel of the Uzi against the guy's ear and spoke quietly, but firmly. "You so much as pass gas and I'll pop your head like a ripe melon."

The shooter froze.

"Now, nice and easy . . . let the rifle fall from your grip."

The shooter complied.

"Good boy. Now slide one arm at a time behind your back. Get cute and it's never-never land for you."

The shooter did what Marc told him to do.

Marc grabbed a heavy nylon restraining tie from his musette bag. He laid the Uzi on the small of the guy's back and slid the tie around the shooter's wrist, then he slid the pointed end through the slot and pulled it tight. Then he took the man's handkerchief from a hip pocket and made a gag out of it. He placed it over the guy's mouth and tied it off behind his head. One more tie from the musette bag went around the shooter's legs at the ankles. Marc checked his work and whispered once more to the startled man. "You be a real good boy until I get back and I'll consider not blowing your brains all over this hillside. If you're not in exactly the same position I leave you in, when I get back, hell's gonna have another inductee. You got all that?"

The shooter's eyes were wide and filled with fear. He nodded.

Marc reached over the guy's head and took the M-16. He dropped the magazine and checked the remaining firepower through the witness holes. He frisked the bound shooter and found two more thirty-round sticks for the auto gun. He took a fresh one and crammed it up the well. "Thanks," he said. "I'll be back."

Marc slung the Uzi over his shoulder on its sling

and cradled the M-16. "Hey, bro," Marc said. "I got the third shooter."

"Yeah, so I heard," Carl replied.

"I'm gonna give these other two a chance to surrender. If that doesn't work, I'll give 'em a little excitement. You might have to burn 'em with the Stinger. Stay ready."

"Say the word and I'll send out the hornets," Carl replied.

Marc moved through the weeds toward the other shooters. They were lying quietly in the weeds now, their assault weapons silent. He slipped through the tall weeds and grass with the cunning of a cat preparing for a dinner of field mice. He crouched low, the M-16 ready to spit 5.56mm death. When he found the position he liked, he stopped, checked the area around him as carefully as he could in the darkness, and made his move. "Hey, assholes . . . you lookin' for me?"

The startled shooters turned almost in tandem. Their weapons came on line and they started to fire. Then they saw Marc in the glow from the fire below and they froze.

"Well, I'm impressed. Yeah, I'll tell you, it sure takes a real man to ambush somebody. You must be super-tough guys. I'm sure your mothers would be proud. Now, unless you want me or the real angry guy in the rig to make sausage out of your butts, lay those weapons down very slowly. You can be brave if you feel lucky. You might even kill me. Of course, if you do, the man in the truck watching us on the infrared scanner is gonna chop you into so many pieces you won't even make good dog food . . . just like he did the first two hotshots. Now what's it gonna be . . . you wanna quit or do you wanna die?"

"Why don't you answer that question, hero?" a cold voice asked from behind Marc. And then a gun barrel jabbed into his right kidney from the rear and Marc instinctively froze.

# Chapter Eleven

□ □ □

Frank struggled to load Dermont Ashland into the sleeper of the Kenworth tractor. He tried to be as gentle as he could under the circumstances, but he knew the old man was in severe pain. And if he didn't get medical attention for the old guy very soon, he would surely die. Ashland's condition had seemed to worsen on the road to the Ashland Transportation Services trucking terminal. When he finally got Ashland into the sleeper and covered with a blanket, he noticed a revolver lying on the edge of the mattress. He picked it up and tucked it into his jacket pocket.

Ashland struggled for breath. He looked at Frank through dazed eyes. "Howard, where are we?"

"It's Frank, Mr. Ashland. How are you feeling?"

"Oh, Frank, I'm sorry. I can't see very well. I thought you were Howard. Where is Howard?"

"He's back at the house, sir."

"Oh. Where are we?"

"At the terminal. We're in a rig and I'm going to get us out of this part of the country for a while." Frank noticed the hollow look of Ashland's face. His skin was pale and he seemed to be very cool to the touch.

"What happened? I had a bad dream. I thought

135

something had gotten out of hand and the FBI had arrested us. I'm so glad it was another dream."

Frank hesitated. "It wasn't a dream, Mr. Ashland. The FBI had us, but you collapsed and I shot our way out of the house. The feds will be looking in every corner of this country for us. I was forced to kill six FBI agents back at the house. They aren't going to take that too kindly."

"Then they do know, don't they?" Ashland gasped and choked to get the breath in his lungs.

"They know something. I'm not sure how much. Whatever they know, it was enough for them to get a federal magistrate to sign a warrant. That tells me they know too much. We have to disappear for a little while."

Ashland appeared startled. "How could they know, Frank? There are only a handful of people who know what is really happening here. Even the people who went into the compound didn't know why they were really there. We have a very dangerous leak and I think I know who it is."

"My gut tells me the same thing I think you're thinking. The senator, right?" Frank asked.

"It would have to be. He's the only one who could pull enough federal strings fast enough to get the FBI moving on this." Ashland propped himself up on one elbow. He looked around the cab and then into the dark parking lot of his trucking company. "We have to terminate him, Frank. He must be stopped before he destroys all of it."

"Yes, sir, Mr. Ashland," Frank said. "I think I need to get you to a doctor very soon. It looks like it could be a problem with your heart."

Ashland laughed. "Heavens no, Frank. It isn't my heart, it's asthma. Mine's triggered by excessive excitement and that's one of the reasons I stay so calm at the pony races. It's one of those things I've learned to live with and few people who know me know about my problem with it. It must have been a major attack at the house, because I remember very damned little about it."

Frank spent several minutes explaining the sequence of events as he knew them to Dermont Ashland. When he finished, Ashland stroked his hair and looked into the dark parking lot for a long moment.

"Frank," he said. "We must take first things first. I want to get word to some of the other people we know we can trust. I want the senator hit and I want him hit before noon. If he's talked, this entire project is history. I'll be financially ruined, and if the feds don't kill us, you and me will probably spend the rest of our natural days in a federal correctional facility. And, Frank, that doesn't sit too well with my asthma."

"Mr. Ashland, with all due respect, sir, there are six dead federal agents at your house as we speak. If we chance a hit on the senator tonight, even if he's home, the feds or some other cops could be waiting on us. If the senator is the squealer, then you know he must have federal protection."

"Protection? Hell, man, what protection? He's in this thing up to his honorable executive ass. Unless—"

"Unless what?" Frank asked. He turned around in the driver's seat of the eighteen-wheeler and checked the parking lot. A sixth sense screamed at him that something was wrong. Terribly wrong. Danger was lurking somewhere in the cover of the Kentucky darkness. He could feel it, but he couldn't see it. Yet still, Frank knew it was there.

"Unless he's set me up as his scapegoat and he's planning to carry out the project by himself."

"Okay, superman, lay that rifle down real slow like.

Only reason I ain't killin' you now is 'cause I want to see your face when we take that nuclear thing away from you." The unseen voice from behind was cold, firm, and deliberate.

Marc gently lowered the weapon to the ground. "Who are you people?"

"Boy, you're hardheaded. I got the damn gun stickin' in your ribs. I'll ask the questions," the man said.

"Kill the son of a bitch, Calvin," one of the shooters who had been lying on the ground said.

"Calvin, you're outnumbered. There's no possible way for you to get away from this place alive," Marc said.

"Like hell there ain't. We gonna travel in style in that super machine you're drivin'. Hell, boy, we might even let you do the drivin' for us. Whatta you think about that, Donnie?"

Donnie didn't hesitate. "I think we ought to kill this asshole. He's gonna cause us a lotta grief, Calvin. Whatta you say, Les?"

Les broke his silence. "Yeah, Cav'in, he's right. The bastard's done seen us. They done smashed that helicopter and tore the shit outta two of Mr. Ashland's best tankers. I b'lieve like Donnie, we ought to take care of this un and go down yonder and wipe that nigger out, then get our asses outta here. I b'lieve we done bit into some serious shit. Old man Ashland and Frank didn't say nothin' 'bout a truck with ass-kickin' missiles on it. Look what they done to them two foreigners. Why, they never knowed what hit 'em."

"That's enough. Both of you. We got to find that gizmo and get outta Dodge. This one knows where they got it hid. I want it. That foreign fella that hired me said we had to get it and give it to his foreign buddies if we wanna get paid. I don't know about you, but I'd sure as hell like to get my money for this deal."

Donnie spoke up and looked around in the darkness. "Hey, where's Jim?"

"He was over by the edge down thataway last time I seen him," Les said.

Donnie stepped forward and crammed the barrel of his M-16 into Marc's face. "Hey, hardcase . . . did you kill our friend Jim?"

"You'll never know," Marc said softly. He moved with his left foot and threw a perfect front snap kick into Donnie's testicles. He spun in the same movement, knocked the barrel of Calvin's weapon off line, and followed that with a sailing open right hand. The heel of the hand caught Calvin at the base of the ear and sent him reeling.

Les fired a wasted burst just as Marc's left foot caught his forearm. He fell back from the intensity of the kick and lost his weapon as he fell. His wasted rounds flew wild.

Marc kicked the M-16 away from Les. The guy scrambled to his feet and Marc caught him in the ribs with a roundhouse kick. Marc continued the spin and stopped abruptly. Les was trying to get to his feet again. Marc moved and faked a left front snap kick. Les shielded himself against the attack, but Marc delivered a right snap kick instead. The big warrior's foot smashed into Les's ribs and sent him to the ground, moaning and gasping for air.

Calvin was up now. He came at Marc and tried to tackle him. Marc moved left. His right foot flew out and caught Calvin at shin level. Calvin mumbled something unintelligible as he fell facefirst into the tall weeds.

Donnie was also up, his hands clutching his family jewels. But then his hands flew from his crotch and came swinging wildly at Marc. A left jab barely missed and Marc ducked low, came around with the butt of his hand, and slammed it into Donnie's face. Blood spurted and Donnie grunted. Then the big goon threw a hard left. Marc ducked, but just in time to catch the backup punch . . . a right hook. Marc's head spun for an instant with little white dots flying sporadically through his vision. He dropped back, his hands up to shield his face. Donnie rushed him, screaming in a mad rage. Marc rolled right. Donnie followed, his arms flailing air and his face bleeding. Marc stopped, spun sideways, and came out of the spin on his feet. He threw a savage roundhouse and it landed boot-first into Donnie's chest. The trucker fell back, but he wasn't stopped. Marc stepped forward and landed a right-left combination into Donnie's face. More blood came and this time Donnie spat out broken teeth.

"That done it, superman," Donnie said. He charged with the ferocity of a raging bull.

Marc sidestepped and slapped the goon on his ears. Donnie stumbled, but he didn't fall. Marc assisted the goon's awkward balance with a swift kick to the seat of the guy's pants. He slammed facefirst into the weeds and took a mouthful of dirt in the process. Marc came in hard for the kill. He hit Donnie with a left boot and followed that with another kick to the head. The big goon gasped and fell flat. He didn't move.

Marc shook off the effects of the hook to the head. He looked around just in time to see Calvin coming at him with a large-blade knife. He blocked the blade with his forearm and grabbed Calvin's massive wrist with his other hand. Calvin grunted and tried to kick, but Marc was too fast. A left knee to the testicles took the wind out of Calvin's sails. He bowed over and grabbed at his testicles. But it wasn't over. Calvin was up, his face etched with burning pain and fierce anger. He swung the knife across Marc's face, barely missing. The gleaming blade slashed thin air as Marc spun once more and kicked Calvin's legs from under him. The oversized thug slammed into the ground flat on his back. Marc jumped on top of him and came around with a right to finish the job. Calvin's body vibrated and then trembled like an erupting volcano. He threw Marc off in a single thrust. Marc landed three feet away. Calvin was on his feet, the knife's razor edge seeking flesh.

Marc moved as the blade slashed through the air again. Then shots rang out and Calvin vibrated like he was holding a live electrical wire. When the vibrations stopped, he fell to the ground like fresh-cut timber.

Marc fell also. He rolled, his right hand seeking the grip of the Smith & Wesson 5906 9mm automatic. He found it and cleared the holster. His finger came back on the double-action trigger and the first shot caught Les in the shoulder. But it didn't do the job. Les got off a burst of 5.56mm hellfire that strafed the ground beside Marc. Dirt and dead grass flew. Marc rolled again and fired, but the shot missed.

Les tapped out another burst and more dirt and debris rained into the night sky.

Marc pointed rather than aimed, and let go a volley of two double-taps. Three of the two pair caught Les in the chest. The fourth split his skull when it passed through the bridge of his nose. Les catapulted backward and the spray of life's blood was silhouetted against the fiery ruins of the eighteen-wheelers on the highway below. Les's legs buckled and he fell. His eyes were open wide. He was dead before he hit the ground.

Marc looked around and checked to see what had happened to Donnie. He was still sprawled out in la-la land, his face snugly against the weeds at the top of the slope. Marc looked around in the weeds for his Icom handheld that had fallen from his belt during the fight.

He couldn't find it, so he felt in his hip pocket for the mini-MagLite flashlight he usually carried there. He found it and used it to locate the Icom. He reconnected the tac harness and made a call to Carl. "Hey, bro, you still on?"

Carl's voice was excited. "Affirmative. What the hell is going on up there? I've tried to call a dozen times. Everything went over the crest and I couldn't see anything on the imager. You okay?"

"Yeah. I got my head jarred a little, but I'm all right. I got two dead up here plus the two you iced from down there. I got two more we need to move to the bottom. They know a few things I think we'll find interesting. Secure the rig, bring some nylon restraints, and come give me a hand."

"Got it. See you in a short. By the way, where'd the fourth one come from?" Carl asked.

"He was on the back side of the hill," Marc replied. "I didn't see him and he got the drop on me. We had some hand-to-hand discussion up here. I'll fill you in later. Right now, we need to get these bad boys into the living quarters and take 'em for a ride before all hell breaks loose down there. Cops can't be too far away and it'll be daylight soon."

Carl watched the image on the hill through the infrared imager until he was satisfied it was Marc. There were no standard code words in the conversation, so Carl realized everything really was all right with Marc at the top of the high-cut slope. He grabbed the nylon restraints, his Uzi, and his musette bag and left the cab. He walked slowly toward the slope and stared up toward Marc. "Affirmative on your last transmission. I'm comin' your way. I like it when we can have a conversation with stubborn bad boys . . . especially when I know they got answers."

* * *

Jon was very nervous. Although he had been a mercenary most of his adult life, he knew that eventually death would come to claim him. But this—dying in a dark hole hundreds of feet beneath the earth—wasn't his idea of a respectable merc death. And in his profession, dying with honor and dignity was a paramount issue.

Dr. Caldwell scanned panel meters, indicator lights, and warning systems in order to determine the extent of the leak inside Containment Unit 1. She, too, was feeling the stress of a potential leak. She, perhaps better than anyone still alive in the facility, realized the deadly potential of the materials stored in the isolation storage units. A leak, even a minor one, could spell disaster for thousands . . . perhaps millions. Should the material, especially some of the bacteriological kind, escape into the general atmosphere at the top, there would be neither a way to warn of impending death nor any way to stop it. And right now, that was something she's rather not have to deal with. As far as problems were concerned, she recognized that her proverbial cup was running over.

"How bad is it?" Jon asked harshly.

Dr. Caldwell didn't dignify his question by even looking up. She kept her eyes trained on the instrumentation that lined the walls outside of the containment unit.

"Dammit, woman, I asked you a question," Jon said angrily. He grabbed Caldwell by her right arm and jerked her upright against him.

"I don't know. An accurate evaluation can't be made from out here. Someone has to go inside and make a physical inspection. If it's serious, we could have irreversible problems."

"Cut the bullshit. How bad is it?" Jon asked. His voice was unsympathetic.

"I suggest you go inside and check it for yourself. You seem to be the one here who has an answer for everything."

Jon backhanded Dr. Caldwell and knocked her to her knees. "I'm going to kill you . . . remember that."

Caldwell looked up at Jon from the floor and laughed. "If there's a leak in that room, you'd better kill me soon. If you don't, the materials in there will. The only problem I see with that is you're going to die, too. Rather comforting, isn't it?"

Jon stepped back. "You had better hope that you are not lying to me. If I find out you are, I'll cut your heart out."

Caldwell refused to back off. "You're a strange one. You remind me of a flunky baseball pitcher. You're all windup and no pitch."

"Are you going inside to make an inspection?"

Dr. Caldwell rose to her feet and smiled. "Yes, would you like to come with me?"

"No, I'll watch through the window."

"You're a man overwhelmed with courage, Jon. I can see why your country would be proud of you."

Jon drew his hand back to smack Dr. Caldwell again, but he held it. "I'm growing very tired of your attitude. Get that suit on, and get your ass in there."

Dr. Caldwell said, "When I go in, I'm going to enter through the airlocks. If there is a leak, and those locks are violated or damaged by another tremor, whatever is inside there floating around in the air will be released into the air supply for the compound. That airlock must not be tampered with in any way. Can you get that through your thick head?"

Jon's face drew tight. "I will see that it is not bothered."

"If there is something leaking in there and you and your friends want to live, I suggest you do just that," Dr. Caldwell said coldly. She stepped away from the equipment and entered the decontamination unit across the hallway. "When I go inside here, I am going to set the airlocks and enter through the overhead airlock tunnel. If there's something you want to say, do it now or keep your mouth shut." Caldwell paused for a long moment. "Well, is there?"

"No," Jon said. "Just get in there and find the leak."

"Good," Caldwell said. She entered the door and closed it behind her. She set the heavy steel bars across it and closed the vaultlike tumblers to make it perfectly secure. Then she chose a pressurized suit and climbed into it. She set the seals and turned on the portable air supply on the backpack through the valve on the front. When the suit pressurized, she sealed the head gear. Then she looked through the heavy, three-inch glass and pointed to the overhead tunnel so Jon would know what she was doing. She climbed the narrow ladder and disappeared inside the tunnel. In less than a minute, she reappeared on the other side inside Containment Unit 1.

Jon watched through the window, scrutinizing every move she made.

Dr. Caldwell checked the hallway entrance door first. She secured the tumblers, set the bar, and verified the pressure seal. Then she moved among the racks of canisters that filled the room. She inspected them one row at a time until she finally reached the back portion of the room. There, she lifted a canister marked NERVE GAS and set it on the floor. She removed the security seal and opened the regulator valve until the substance filled the room with a mist that vanished before it trailed too far skyward. The mist came from the propellant gases used to dispense the nerve gas from the container.

When the canister was empty, she moved to the back wall of the containment unit and pressed a series of switches that activated the automatic airlock doors throughout the facility. An alarm sounded and all doors immediately closed, locked, and pressurized.

Jon panicked. He saw the doors close the instant the alarm sounded and he realized he was trapped in a narrow hallway, separated from his men. He beat on the heavy, thick glass, but it did him no good.

Dr. Caldwell moved past the switches and opened a small airlock door that led out the back of the containment unit. When she was safely out of the room, she closed the door, twisted the tumbler lock, and set the heavy steel bar. She was outside of the room now and into a narrow service tunnel that only she and Dr. von Wirth knew about. She had just used and secured the only entrance possible from inside the facility.

She walked for a hundred feet inside the tunnel and came to a ladder that led straight up into darkness. She leaned her head back and looked. "Damn, I must be nuts," she said aloud, and then she started climbing toward the surface of the earth. And with each step up the ladder, she left the doers of evil to mankind a little farther behind in man-made hell.

# Chapter Twelve

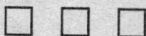

□ □ □

Marc pressed the button on the intercom and called to Carl in the living quarters of the Leeco trailer. "There's a truckstop five miles ahead. I'm going to shut down for a while and we can have that conversation we promised Jim and Donnie."

"Sounds good," Carl replied. "They're both sittin' back here enjoyin' the ride. I don't think they're too pleased with the hospitality. They haven't said much for the last two hours."

"Yeah, well, there's a lot of sadness in the world," Marc said. "If they think the hospitality is weak now, wait until we get this machine stopped and I get back there for the discussion. Boy, talk about inhospitable. Wow."

Carl watched Jim and Donnie's faces when Marc's voice came across the intercom speaker. Both men tensed and Carl could see the nervous anticipation building inside them. Donnie tried to stay cool, but Carl knew the fat lip the guy had and the cut across his left cheek hurt. Carl could tell by the expression on Donnie's face that he had no desire for a second dose of the same medicine. Jim hadn't spoken since Carl had strapped him in the chair where he sat, but the guy's eyes were still open wide as if he were in shock.

Marc squinted his eyes against the early-dawn light. To his left, the sun crept slowly and as if deliberately over the Blue Ridge Mountains with gentle fingers of glittering light that sparkled on the roadside as it bounced off of dew-kissed foliage. Aside from its inherent beauty, the sparkling light had two meanings for him. It meant he would be better able to see another block of attackers if they came, and it meant that he was late on his schedule for Huntsville. That he hadn't heard any follow-up information from General Rogers bothered him. Rogers and Brittin Crain were usually on the tip top of things in the Power City, but something didn't feel right about the situation now. Worse yet, something was very strange about the entire operation, had been from the onset. That thought plagued Marc and wouldn't let go.

Something was very, very wrong.

The exit sign for the truckstop came into view and Marc made the lane change to prepare to exit. He scanned the mirrors for traffic behind him and looked ahead to be sure everything was clear. It was, so he slowed the Leeco rig and gave a signal to exit. He coasted the big rig to the end of the exit ramp and turned left toward the truckstop. When he reached the entrance, he gave a left signal and entered the parking lot. When he reached the end of the truck lines, he found a vacant space near the very back of the huge lot. He pulled the rig alongside another eighteen-wheeler and shut off the giant diesel power plant.

He scanned the parking lot and felt relieved that nothing looked out of place or suspicious. Then he tapped the intercom button and spoke to Carl. "We're here, bro. Soon as I secure everything, I'll be back to see if either of our inhospitable guests can imitate a songbird. You need anything from the cab before I come back?"

"Nope, I can't think of a thing. I have one thought, though."

"What's that?" Marc asked.

"You might want to consider leaving the rig idling to help muffle any sound from back here in case these guys start screaming too loudly when we begin the questioning." Carl looked at Jim and Donnie and smiled broadly.

"Good idea. We wouldn't want anyone who happened to be walking too close to get the wrong idea. It could get nasty back there. I'll follow your advice."

"We're waitin'," Carl said. He looked at Jim and Donnie and smiled broadly again.

Marc left the cab, secured it, and walked to the rear of the trailer. He hit the combination on the security transmitter and the hydraulic doors opened. He climbed in, closed the doors, and worked his way toward the front of the trailer and the living-quarters area. He hit the proper code on the transmitter again, and the door to the control room and living quarters opened automatically. He walked in, mean-faced, stopped, and stared at Jim and Donnie. "Party time, boys."

Neither man moved.

"Hey, bro, don't hurt 'em yet. Give 'em a chance," Carl said. They often played the good cop–bad cop routine and it was his turn to be the good guy.

"Sure, I'll give 'em a chance just like the one they gave us when we topped that hill or when we came back to that burning wreckage. Damn straight, I'll give 'em a chance," Marc said.

"I don't know, man. If you're too hard on 'em . . . I mean don't go and kill these guys or anything. We left enough bodies back there on that hillside.

They'll talk. Right guys?" Carl looked at Jim and Donnie and nodded his head.

"Man, I don't know what you want us to talk about," Donnie said.

"Maybe I can give you a few clues," Marc said. "First, who do you work for?"

Jim looked at Donnie and they stared at each other for a long moment.

"Ashland Transportation Services out of Kentucky. We're truck drivers. I swear it," Jim said, his voice was trembling.

"Truck drivers!" Marc yelled. "Truck drivers carrying M-16s and ambushing another trucker from the top of a ridge. Setting up a roadblock to crash rigs on an interstate highway. Don't expect me to buy this truck-driver shit." He reached to the small of his back and came out with his Smith & Wesson 5906. "I'm gonna do it now and be done with it. We can dump their bodies at a rest area somewhere. I don't have time for this crap."

Carl jumped up and gently grabbed the end of the Smith's barrel and pushed it slowly toward the floor. "Now easy, bro. You're movin' too fast. If we kill 'em now, we'll have to haul their bodies all day in the rig. I don't like that. It's too risky. How about it, guys? You want to answer the man's questions. He's tired and he isn't real strong on patience."

Jim and Donnie sat silently, their faces etched with fear.

"All right," Marc said. "One more chance. I want to know everything. Who you work for. Why you want to kill us. Who the foreigners were. Tell me everything and tell it fast. I'm not in the mood for this crap." Marc racked the slide back on the Smith and let it slam closed. The hammer stayed back and he touched his finger to the trigger. "This is your last chance."

Donnie looked at Jim, his swelling face pale from fear. "We better tell this man what he wants to know or I think he's gonna kill us, Jim."

"Yeah, well, old man Ashland or Frank will kill us if we tell him."

"We got to have some guarantee of some kind of protection. The old man would kill us for talkin'," Donnie said.

Carl smiled coldly and gestured toward Marc. "This man is going to kill you if you don't talk. Seems to me you boys got your asses between the proverbial rock and a hard place."

Jim was shaking now. "Let's tell 'em, Donnie. What say?"

Donnie sat silent, his face on the barrel of the Smith & Wesson in Marc's hands. He looked up at Marc and his shoulders drooped. He took a deep breath, then let it out. His voice was soft and weak. "I don't see that we got much of a choice. What do you want to know?"

Marc's face hardened. He leveled the barrel of the Smith at Donnie's face. His grip was firm and his aim, steady. He spoke between clenched teeth. "I want to know every damned thing there is too know about why you wanted to kill my partner and me. You'd better be damned convincing and you'd better not leave out one important detail. Not one."

Dr. Caldwell hid low in the under brush at the top of the hill a quarter of a mile from the old barn used for the entrance into the underground facility. She had removed the pressurized suit and hidden it beneath leaves and grass in the edge of the woods. She knew she had to get to help and do it quickly, but she was very afraid. From her vantage point, she could see thick smoke towering from the inferno that had once been the mission control center. She surmised from her observation that the tremor had been caused by an intense explosion at the center, probably precipitated by some of Jon's comrades. And that thought was not comforting.

Below her, at the mission control center, security personnel swarmed around a large truck, or at least the skeleton of what appeared to have been a truck. She wasn't sure. The thought occurred to her that the men in uniform might not all be security people. Perhaps Jon's organization had infiltrated their ranks also. And if they had, what were her alternatives?

She tried to control both her rage and her fear. She realized she was dressed awkwardly for a day of hiding in the wooded areas of the huge compound, but she was scared to do anything else until she had devoted adequate time to studying her predicament.

Caldwell's first thought was that she needed to get to a telephone and contact the FBI or military intelligence. But how?

Surely, she thought, if she were seen running around the compound in her nightgown, her credibility would sink to an all-time low. But at this moment in her life, credibility wasn't the issue, survival was.

She knew she had taken a grave chance by releasing chemical agents into the air inside the containment unit. Particles of the compound had surely clung to her suit when she escaped through the hatch at the rear of the room. There was no possible chance that anyone could follow her. The hatches had been designed to permit locking from either side, with neither side able to unsecure the other. That meant that Jon and his cronies were effectively sealed inside the facility until they were able to get the elevator running again. And, she hoped, she could get to the authorities before that happened.

Caldwell sat for over an hour watching the action

around the center. Everything in sight seemed to be in total chaos. People and equipment with flashing lights were everywhere. She hadn't seen so many people in all the years she had worked at Marshall. And certainly somewhere in the midst of all the authorities, there had to be one person she could identify and trust.

Then it occurred to her. "Damn," she said. "Caldwell, you idiot, why didn't you think of this before? Of course, it was too damned simple!"

She made her way through the woods and worked around the center for almost an hour. Then it was within sight: the shuttle-bus parking area. Her car. And in her car was the cellular telephone. If she could get to that without being seen, she could call the FBI.

Caldwell stopped and caught her breath at the edge of the woods. Her car was seventy-five yards away and the distance from her to it was all open ground. No cover. No turning back.

She looked hard around the area and saw no one. She said a short prayer, took a deep breath, and ran for her life.

Frank couldn't hold it any longer, he had to go to the bathroom. Dermont Ashland was sleeping comfortably in the sleeper while white lines drifted by the rig like arrows shot from a compound bow. He saw the sign on the side of the highway that indicated the truckstop three miles ahead. Frank moved the rig into the right lane and waited for the exit. When it appeared, he slowed as he approached the ramp and made the exit. He stopped at the end of the ramp at the stop sign and turned right.

The truckstop was a half a mile off the interstate. Frank turned into the lot, stopped the rig, and left it idling. He looked back into the sleeper at Dermont

Ashland. The old man was sound asleep. Frank decided to try to awaken him. He spoke softly at first. "Mr. Ashland, wake up. We're at a truckstop in Tennessee. I'm making a pit stop if you need to go to the can or anything."

There was no response.

Frank tried again. "Mr. Ashland, pit stop. You need to go to the can?"

Nothing.

"Huh," Frank said. "Maybe next time." He opened the cab door and climbed from the big tanker. He hit the ground and walked quickly across the parking lot to the restaurant. When he got inside, he followed the arrows and found the rest room. It felt like the greatest relief he had ever known.

Frank returned to the parking lot and walked back to the overroad tanker rig. He climbed up and opened the door. Ashland was still sleeping soundly, so Frank made himself comfortable behind the wheel and dropped the rig into gear. He headed for the highway again . . . for Huntsville.

The first sedan seemed to materialize from out of nowhere. It sped past the front of the Kenworth tractor and cut in short and hard, then skidded to a stop.

Frank slammed on the brakes as an automatic reaction. The big rig groaned and decelerated, but there was no way to stop. Impact was only a few feet away.

It didn't happen. Just when Frank thought he would collide with the crazy man in the gray sedan, the car lurched to life and spun out of the rig's path.

"Shit!" Frank yelled. He crammed the rig into another gear and floored the accelerator.

A second sedan appeared. This one was behind him. He heard the roar of the engine before he actually saw the car. It pulled alongside the rig, tires screaming and the rear end fishtailing as it gained speed. Frank shifted his senses into full survival mode. His heart rate shot upward as he fought the rig with every ounce of strength in his body. He pressed harder on the accelerator, but it was on the floor as far as it would go.

An excited voice blared over a public-address system in the car beside him. "Montino, this is the FBI. Stop the truck now and you won't be harmed," the harsh voice said.

"Not in this lifetime," Frank mumbled. He cut hard left and tried to sideswipe the sedan to force it off the road.

The driver of the sedan saw the move coming and swerved left into the oncoming lane. Another car, a red BMW, was approaching, this one an innocent passerby. The driver didn't see the sedan and truck tangling until the last possible second. That driver cut hard right and panicked. The BMW hit the shoulder and the frightened driver lost control. The car spun around three or four times and slammed into a guardrail.

Frank didn't care what happened to the guy in the BMW. He turned his attention to the sedan. It was back alongside now with something he couldn't understand blaring over the PA. He looked in his right mirror and saw the first sedan coming hard on him along the right shoulder of the highway. Now there were lights, red and blue, flashing in the grilles of both cars. The entrance ramp to the interstate highway was just ahead. The sedan on the left was trying to overtake the rig now to block entrance onto the ramp. Frank cut into it hard again. The driver swerved left and avoided the collision.

Frank shot another glance into the rearview mirror on the right. The first sedan was alongside there now. He was closing, also trying to overtake the rig. There was a man there, leaning from the passenger's window with a handgun in his extended right hand. He was aiming toward the tanker's front end.

Frank swerved right and the sound of metal grinding against metal screeched through the air. The rig sustained the collision with moans, groans, and a thunderous jolt.

Dermont Ashland shot upright in the sleeper. He rubbed his eyes and felt the rig swerve erratically. The force of the sudden turn caused him to slam back down against the mattress. He yelled loudly. "Frank, what is going on? What's happening? Are you all right?"

Frank didn't bother to look back at Ashland. He yelled instead. "Feds. They've found us."

Ashland felt faint. He sat up again and stared through the windshield. "Where, Frank? Where are they?"

"On the sides. One on each side and closing hard on us. Hold on."

Frank cut the rig onto the entrance ramp. The machine strained under the sudden motion. The chemical load sloshed forward, then sideways. The giant rig leaned hard to the right and the left tires came off of the pavement for a second, then dropped back down.

The feds were still there, sirens screaming now and the lights in their grilles flashing a warning. The first sedan popped in and out of view on the right side and the second one stayed in view on the left.

The ramp narrowed ahead just before entry onto the highway. Frank glanced into the mirrors to try to get a look at oncoming traffic on the interstate highway. He could see little except the sedan and the men who called themselves FBI agents.

Ashland panicked. "What are we going to do, Frank?"

"Outrun the mothers. If we can't outrun them, then

we'll outshoot them. Just stay calm and hold on. You'll be safe in the sleeper."

"They know it all, Frank. They know about the project. We're destroyed. All the research at Huntsville is destroyed. We're doomed."

"It's not over until the last shot is fired, Mr. Ashland. And we ain't done shooting," Frank screamed. He steered the rig onto the highway and ran a woman in a Toyota off the road in the process. The woman sounded her car horn, but Frank ignored it and grabbed another gear.

The second sedan from the left shot past the woman in the Toyota and tried to overtake the rig again.

It didn't work.

Frank swerved across both southbound lanes and slammed into his pursuer. The rig rocked again with the heart-stopping sound of metal chewing metal.

Ashland screamed from the sleeper, "You're going to kill us, Frank. Do something."

"I *am* doing something. *I'm* not going to kill us, *they* are. Just hang on back there. A passenger car is no match for thirty-five tons of tractor-trailer. They can't win."

The first sedan streaked alongside the rig. Traffic fanned out in erratic directions as the rig and the sedans wove a course of death down the interstate highway. Four pops sounded on the right side and the dull thud of lead devouring metal resonated through the rig.

"They're shooting at us, Frank," Ashland screamed.

Frank felt the rig list to the right. "They've hit one of the tires. We've got a flat on the right side."

"What now?" Ashland screamed.

"We get nasty," Frank replied. He cut hard into the sedan to the right. He hit, metal screeching and grinding. He jerked left for an instant and swerved hard right once more. He slammed the sedan broadside and the driver tried to maintain control.

Shots rang out on the left now. A shooter fired into the front of the ATS rig. Hot lead penetrated aluminum and harmlessly spent its energy.

Frank cut back hard to the left now. He impacted the sedan with the brave shooter and knocked it onto the shoulder. Ahead, a line of traffic rolled south, oblivious to the melee occurring behind them.

Frank accelerated. The diesel engine whined under the strain and black smoke thundered skyward from the twin stacks. He looked right and the agents were beside him again. And now there was more trouble. Two state police cars were in on the action. They closed from the rear, weaving their way through the traffic that had dissipated in the wake of the speeding rig.

More shots rang out from the left. The agent was firing at the front of the rig again.

Frank swerved the ATS tanker and slapped into the sedan again. The agent lost control and spun sideways off the shoulder of the road into the median. But now the troopers were on the rear of the ATS rig, their sirens blaring. One of the troopers accelerated, ran to the left shoulder of the highway, and shot past the ATS machine. He cut back onto the pavement and sped ahead. His emergency equipment screamed a warning as he tried to clear traffic before the speeding tanker reached it.

The highway dipped down a quarter of a mile ahead. Beyond that, a long steep grade dropped into a river valley with a long bridge spanning a lake. The trooper was still in the front, but now there were three eighteen-wheelers there also. Frank hadn't seen them until he started down the long grade and now he was closing on them fast.

The trooper shot past the eighteen-wheeler in the

rear. But as he overtook the second one, the driver overreacted and slammed on his brakes. The big rig went into a skid and snaked from one side of the road to the other. The trooper lost control of his car and slammed into the guardrail. Then the driver of the second rig lost it. The big rig jackknifed, turned sideways, and rolled over and over in the highway.

The rig bringing up the rear had nowhere to go. He hit his brakes in a futile effort to stop, but his rig plowed into the rolling eighteen-wheeler and a massive fireball filled the highway.

Frank hit his brakes, looked into the mirrors, and saw the feds sliding broadside. He yelled at Ashland: "It's over!" Then the ATS rig entered the smoking fireball on the highway. Frank closed his eyes, held his breath, and the big ATS tanker filled with benzene collided with the first two eighteen-wheelers. The fireball became a cataclysmic tower of flames that shot high into the sky and rocked the earth with the intensity of the mammoth explosion.

# Chapter Thirteen

□ □ □

"Barnburner, this is Pathfinder. Over." Marc released the push-to-talk switch on the Icom and waited for a reply to come across the ComSat-D communications link. He sat in the passenger's seat while Carl drove the Leeco overroad rig.

Carl watched the highway ahead, but he glanced quickly over at Marc. "Do you believe everything Jim and Donnie said?"

Marc rubbed his chin and stared through the windshield. "I don't know how much to believe. They were accurate on everything to the time we caught them. They knew about the first hitter in the rig and the clown in the chopper. Face it, bro, their information is all we have to go on. What they said makes sense."

"Yeah, but military people and a senator involved in this? Sounds too bizarre for me," Carl quipped. "What could a group of people like that possibly have to gain?"

"Pathfinder, this is Barnburner. Are you there, men?" General Rogers's voice crackled across the Icom speaker.

"Roger, General," Marc said. "Go ahead with your traffic."

"Things have escalated very quickly, Marc," Rogers

said. "We have six dead federal agents in Louisville. I'm going to give you the *Reader's Digest* version of all this. You might want to select your audio tape and make a permanent record of it. Over."

Marc glanced toward Carl. "Six dead feds . . . huh? Jim and Donnie are gaining credibility by the moment." Marc activated the tape-recording system in the Leeco trailer to record both sides of the conversation with General Rogers. He lifted the microphone to his mouth and keyed the Icom transmitter. "Audio tape is rolling, General. What happened in Louisville?"

"No one knows for sure. Everything is just speculation now. Looks like a shoot-out. The agents went there to question Ashland. The Bureau is tracing the identity of a man found there. All we know is he doesn't appear to be American. Agents are also still questioning those two you left at the truckstop for them. So far, the information checks out."

"What about the senator?" Marc asked.

"Brittin told me fifteen minutes ago that agents were on their way to his house in Alexandria. We'll see what he has to say if they find him. There is also a team of men on the way to the senator's home in Kentucky. If the information you have proves accurate to the letter, we have a major problem on our hands. How long will it take you to get to Huntsville?"

"I figure ETA to be around three this afternoon. We're moving as fast as we can," Marc replied.

The tone of Rogers's voice across the speaker was a strong indication of the severity of the problem. "We need you there as soon as possible. We don't know the extent of the damages from the explosion. If that changes the launch schedule for the shuttle, we have us a major baby-sitting job with that contraption you're hauling."

"Affirmative," Marc replied. "Those two guys we

questioned said nothing about blowing up the center until after the shuttle was airborne. What are we missing here, General?"

"I don't know where the other pieces lie, Marc. I just got off the horn with the Boss and I know he's very upset. There have been lives lost in Huntsville and a lot of taxpayers' dollars have gone up in smoke . . . literally. He wants this thing brought to a head and concluded quickly. You and Carl seem to be in for more than any of us bargained for. Accept my apology for that. Over."

"Affirmative, Barnburner. No apology necessary. We're used to it. Over."

"Stand by, Pathfinder. I have Crain on the horn now. Additional intelligence is coming in. Over."

"Roger, Barnburner. Pathfinder, standing by," Marc said. He lowered the microphone and glanced over at Carl as the rig rolled down the interstate highway. "I just can't figure why anyone would want to take control of a space shuttle—if Jim and Donnie knew what they were talking about. There's a lot more to it than we're being told. Some critical piece of information is missing and I can't put a finger on what it is. Any ideas?"

"Got me, bro," Carl said. "Maybe if they can find Ashland or the senator, we can get some answers."

"Yeah," Marc agreed. "We might find the answer waiting in the smoke and ruins at Huntsville. One thing bothers me now."

"What's that?" Carl asked.

"If Huntsville is in ruins, why haven't we been diverted to another location? Why not take the reactor to Houston or the Cape? That doesn't make sense to me. How 'bout you?"

"Does sound strange, doesn't it?"

"If Ashland and his cronies wanted the reactor, why

did they go to all the trouble to do something foolish like blow a building at Marshall? Why not just wait until we got there with the thing and make a hit then? My gut tells me there is something else at Marshall these people were after."

"Possible," Carl said.

The Icom speaker crackled with General Rogers's voice. "Pathfinder, this is Barnburner. I have an update. Crain is coming on the line in a few seconds. He has a field agent in Huntsville who is interviewing a young female research scientist named Dr. Kathleen Caldwell. She claims there is a chemical and bacteriological research laboratory beneath the ground at Marshall and it is under siege. Stand by, Pathfinder. Brittin, are you on with us?"

Marc's lifelong friend and the Highway Warriors' bureaucratic liaison, Brittin Crain, answered immediately. "Roger, General. Hi, guys. General Rogers is correct. I have Special Agent Dennis Hargrove on the phone. He has a young woman in his office who claims that a chemical and biological research laboratory at Marshall has been overtaken by foreign and domestic hostiles who want to steal some of the weapons stored there. This one sounds a little bizarre to me, guys. What's the consensus on the line?"

"You first, Marc," Rogers said.

Marc sat silent for a moment while he contemplated his answer. He looked over at Carl. "Now it's making sense. Ashland didn't want the damned reactor, he wants the chem/bac canisters in that facility. That is, if the laboratory really exists. This reactor is a diversion. A damned diversion to get focus off of his mission."

"Bingo," Carl said.

Marc keyed the microphone. "Guys, this is making sense. Ashland never wanted the reactor. He wanted a diversion to get attention off of his real purpose and that was theft of the chemicals and bacteriological weapons there. My question is how a man who runs a trucking company and a financial empire in Louisville, Kentucky, knew about a laboratory at Marshall. Does the government have any record of this lab?"

Crain's voice crackled over the speaker. "Computer is going into that now. We'll have an answer in a few minutes if it isn't buried too deep in the bureaucratic archives. So let me get this straight. You guys think this woman might be legitimate?"

"It would make sense," Marc said. "Think about it. This guy would have no logical reason to tamper with the space shuttle. I'd like to have more background on him and I'd like to meet him face-to-face if you can find him."

"Oh, we've found him," Crain said. "Problem is, we can't get him stopped. Some men from the Bureau were in pursuit on I-65 in Tennessee. Ashland and his right-hand man, Frank Montino, crashed through a blazing wreck on the highway and managed to escape just a few minutes ago. He's somewhere near Huntsville now, would be my guess. They were last seen in an Ashland Transportation Services tanker rig. The rig they're driving is hauling an undiluted load of benzene. They're in a mobile bomb if they come into contact with the wrong kind of firepower."

"Where is the woman now?" Marc asked.

"At the Huntsville field office," Crain replied.

"Keep her where she will be absolutely safe. I want to have some conversation with her when we get to Huntsville. While we are en route, assemble everything you've got on this situation. I'd like it all transmitted to the computer for a hardcopy before we stop at Marshall. What's the shuttle schedule?"

"As far as I know, they're waiting for you. My

information says they can't or won't launch without your cargo. I've heard nothing different," Crain said. "Do you have any news on that, General?"

"Nothing," Rogers said.

"Does this doctor know how many people are in the laboratory?" Marc asked.

"At least twelve, she thinks," Crain replied. "She said there might be more, but she had seen that many. They've allegedly killed most of the people who work in the lab. She speculates that the main man, a Dr. Klaus von Wirth, is in on the deal. We're running him now also. I'll pass that along when we have it. Over."

"Okay," Marc said. "Assemble what you can and get it to us. We're rolling these eighteen wheels as fast as they can go without creating a touchy situation. We'll contact you again when we get to Huntsville. I want to see the doctor as soon as we arrive. Over."

"Roger," Crain said. "If what this woman says is true, there's horror beyond our worst nightmares sitting in canisters beneath the ground at Huntsville. You guys be careful. This one sounds bad."

"Affirmative," Marc said. "The people involved in this haven't seen us create a nightmare yet, but they're about to real soon."

Jon had tried for hours to find a way out of the section of the laboratory that had become his prison. Nothing had worked. Worst of all, his radio didn't work with all of the heavy steel doors closed and locked. When he tried to transmit, the only reply he got was static breaking the squelch. He contemplated his situation and realized there must be a way to get the airlocks to disengage.

The control panel to the containment unit was a maze of LEDs, meters, and switches. Jon didn't know what any of it was and he had no idea how to use it. What he did know was the mission was hours behind schedule and probably in serious jeopardy. Dr. Caldwell hadn't been visible for hours through the thick glass in the wall of the containment unit. He didn't know if she was still inside or if she had found another way out. There was no way he could go inside to check because the doors to the decontamination unit and the containment unit were pressurized and secured from the inside. He sat in the floor in front of the containment-unit control panel and closed his eyes.

The unique sound of the hermetic seal breaking and pressure equalizing caused Jon to snap to attention. He stood and ran to the door that led into the section of the facility where he had left Dr. von Wirth and the other insurgents. Jon twisted the locking handle and the door opened effortlessly. He breathed a deep sigh of relief and ran toward Dr. von Wirth's private lab.

One of the insurgents stopped him. "What the hell happened?"

"Later," Jon scolded. "Get all of the men together and meet back here as quickly as you can. I need a status report on the prisoners and the elevator. We are hours behind schedule. We must get to the top and proceed cautiously lest this mission be lost to failure."

"Yes, sir," the man replied, and disappeared through a doorway.

Jon stopped in front of von Wirth's lab and slowly opened the door. "What happened, doctor? Who shut this place down?"

Von Wirth looked up from a maze of wires protruding from the wall at a panel of switches. "I was hoping you could tell me. Where is Dr. Caldwell?"

"She entered the number-one containment unit wearing one of those special suits. I haven't seen her since. She released something into the room that appeared misty and then she disappeared. Is there a way out of that unit other than the tunnel across the top and the doorway at the window?"

Von Wirth smiled. "Dr. Caldwell is a brilliant mind. She remembered the escape tunnel. She and I are the only people in this facility who know of it. If you haven't seen her since she entered the unit, she is probably in the arms of safety miles from Redstone."

Jon's face showed a puzzled look. "Redstone?" he asked.

"I'm sorry, that's what it was called when I first came to this place. They call it Marshall now, don't they? You will forgive me?"

"How did the doors open?" Jon asked.

Von Wirth gestured to the bundle of wires hanging from the control box on the wall. "I manipulated the wiring in here and reset the pressurization valves. That was a safety device we included in the design of this facility in the unlikely event we ever had a hazardous leak or spill. There are three places the airlocks can be activated: my office, the containment unit, and the master control room. I should have warned you, but I had forgotten all about the escape tunnel. Old age, I suppose. That is behind us; we must get on with the project."

"Can we use this tunnel to get out of here?" Jon asked. He didn't bother to make an effort at hiding his excitement.

Von Wirth laughed and shook his head. "Probably not. Dr. Caldwell most likely left the containment unit contaminated with poisonous gases. She is diligent in her work. She surely secured the doorway from the containment unit once she was on the outside in the tunnel."

"Is there another entry into this tunnel?"

"No," von Wirth said. "I'm afraid not."

"Where does the tunnel lead?"

"Oh," von Wirth replied, "to the surface by way of a narrow channel and a ladder. It goes straight up. An old man like me couldn't climb it."

"So we're back where we started," Jon said. "We must get the elevator working in order to ever leave this place. Is that correct?"

Von Wirth nodded in agreement.

"Jon," the voice said from the doorway. "We have the elevator in service. What now?"

Jon jerked around quickly. "Assemble everyone. I want all of the personnel from the facility that are alive to be here also. We must move now and move fast."

"Yes, sir. Anything else?" the man asked.

"I want to send a couple men to the surface to evaluate the situation on top. It is possible we have been abandoned, since we have been out of contact for so long. We must reevaluate our mission. Get everyone together and I will go over the new plan."

"Yes, sir," the man said. He turned and disappeared through the doorway toward the elevator.

Jon turned back to von Wirth. "Doctor, I want to have the first group of men take a load of chemical weapons and some of the bacteriological canisters when they go to the surface. If all else fails, they can get out of here with at least that much. Where are the devices?"

Von Wirth walked to the door. "Follow me. I will take you to Containment Unit Two near the rear of the facility. I suggest we forget about the first unit, since Dr. Caldwell probably saw fit to release gases in there. We can accomplish this project with the devices in the second unit."

Jon and von Wirth left the private lab and walked

for several minutes until they reached the rear of the facility. Von Wirth stopped in front of a large glass window and a control panel similar to the one at Containment Unit 1. He inspected the meters, lights, and switches. "Yes," he said. "Everything appears to be in good order. We can enter this unit."

"When?" Jon asked.

"Whenever you are ready," von Wirth replied. "I will disable the alarms and the airlocks for this unit. Once we meet with your people in the front, we can begin to remove these canisters."

"Good. Let's get it done," Jon said, and a small smile crossed his weary face.

Von Wirth worked switches and the door to Containment Unit 2 opened. "There, we are ready."

"Now we will go see the others and be done with this." Jon turned and walked toward the front of the complex and the elevator shaft.

Von Wirth followed.

They reached the front reception area and everyone was gathered just as Jon had ordered. The remaining personnel from the laboratory were huddled in one corner of the room, their hands bound behind their backs.

Jon looked at each frightened face, his eyes locking with each one as he scanned them. "We now have the elevator in service. We will leave this place soon. I want four volunteers to ascend the shaft through the elevator and inspect the situation on the surface. There is a possibility of a serious problem with our timetable. Who will go?"

Jon pointed to four volunteers, one at a time. "Good. Choose a technician for each of you. They will carry your load to the surface. Watch them carefully and bring them back with you when you return. If they give you any trouble, kill them where they stand."

All of the men nodded to indicate they understood.

"Once you have loaded the canisters on the rig, two of you bring the hostages back down here with you. The other two make a recon run through the complex and assess the status of our mission. Are there any questions?"

No one responded.

"Good, then be gone," Jon said.

The four volunteers moved out after each one selected a hostage.

Jon turned his attention back to the remaining insurgents. "Two of you watch the other hostages. Same order. If they try to be heroes, kill them. I want to start a line from the containment unit. All of the hostages will be put to work. Bring all of the canisters from the unit to the elevator area. Relay them to the surface and load them on the trucks when the intelligence unit returns from the top. Any questions?"

Once more, there was no response.

"All right, get on with it," Jon said. "I want this completed in the next thirty minutes."

The insurgents moved out behind the reluctant hostages and disappeared through the doorway toward the back of the facility.

"Doctor, could we go back to your office?" Jon asked.

Once inside, Jon sat at the table and looked around the laboratory. "What has brought mankind to the brink of this kind of destruction, doctor?" Jon asked.

"I'm afraid I don't understand."

"These awesome weapons that kill people and leave buildings and factories intact. These heinous chemicals and bacteria that regenerate faster than a plague. Have we come to this level of hatred in our world?" Jon asked.

"You are a man of the gun, Jon. Perhaps you should answer that. You have not seen the horror I have during the Big War. You have not witnessed the slaughter of millions because one group did not like the politics or the faith of another. Germany was a nightmare when I was a child. I came here to do my work for the good of mankind, not its destruction. Were it not for my friend, Dermont Ashland, mankind might be forced to suffer the insufferable . . . endure the unendurable. You want only the nuclear reactor for your country. That is why you are here. I want to remove these weapons to a place where no man can endanger the entirety of civilization with them. You see, I am a man of conscience. I created these devices and made them a reality. Dermont Ashland and Senator Sam Whitten kept this operation running for years after the United States government shut off the funding. We don't exist in this laboratory as far as the government is concerned. We haven't for years."

"But what of the killing power of these things?" Jon asked.

"Yes, killing power. Of course." Von Wirth stroked his hair and smiled. "We have incredible killing power. Our nuclear arsenal is astounding. But these weapons . . . our enemies would be foolish to confront anyone with weapons as powerful as these. If some of these compounds were unleashed in a given area, Jon, there would be no survivors. Not one. I can guarantee that. Even the dreaded neutron bomb is inferior to the potential of the weapons stored in this laboratory."

"Jon." The voice came from the hallway.

Jon turned and looked at the source of the voice. "Yes?"

"The first load is on its way up the elevator."

Jon turned back to von Wirth. "Perhaps another day we shall have time to pursue our innermost thoughts, doctor. But now we must both get on about our business if we are to finish this project."

"Yes, perhaps," Dr. von Wirth said. "Provided those canisters are handled correctly. If they aren't, it is possible there will be no other days for any of us."

# Chapter Fourteen

□ □ □

Frank knew everyone with a badge and a gun would be looking for him and Dermont Ashland. He couldn't believe it when the rig actually cleared the wreckage without exploding into a million pieces. But one thing was certain: an ATS tanker with black soot all over it wouldn't be difficult for anyone to spot on the interstate highway. That's why Frank took the first available exit and left the superslab. He knew the secondary highway ran parallel to the interstate on the maps he had memorized before the trouble began. With that in mind, he did the last thing the feds or the state police ever thought he would do. He took the secondary road and doubled back to the truckstop where the feds had made him.

Ashland was mentally between shock and a coma. He couldn't believe what had happened on the highway. He couldn't accept the fact that the project was in serious jeopardy and his life was dangling on the end of a frayed thread. But now he was settled somewhat, and he found himself thinking rationally again. "Frank," he said. "We must get to Ardmore, Alabama. If we can get to the warehouse, we will have the resources to move the weapons before anyone can determine what has happened. Can you get us there?"

175

"If you had asked that question an hour ago, Mr. Ashland, my answer would have been positively yes. Now, though, I can't promise you either one of us will be alive one minute from now. Things have changed; the feds know who we are and where we are."

"We must get to the warehouse, Frank. We can establish radio contact with our employees inside the facility from Ardmore. If the links are in place, we can monitor everything that is happening with the shuttle. I'll have ten trucks at the distribution point by seven this evening. When that is accomplished, there will be nothing anyone can do to stop us."

Frank scanned the parking lot before he committed the rig to the right turn into the parking lot. Everything looked normal, but if the feds were watching the lot, things would be that way for cover, if nothing else.

He turned the scorched tanker into the lot. "Now remember what I told you, Mr. Ashland—when I make my move, you must move also. Are you feeling up to it?"

"Well, the asthma is gone, but I'll admit my knees are weak. I'll make myself get over that when the chips fall on the table. You do what you have to do and I'll be all right." Ashland propped himself up on his elbows and gazed through the windshield from the sleeper bay.

Frank looked around the lot very carefully as he moved through the truckstop parking area. "Okay. This is going to require precise timing. If we blow it here, it may be our last shot. No rehearsals. It's got to be right the first time. Are you with me?"

"I understand and I'm with you, Frank," Ashland said reassuringly. "You lead the way and I'll be in your footsteps."

Frank eased the rig through the lines of parked trucks. Then he saw the one he wanted. A Kenworth pulling a refer drove away from the fuel pumps and headed toward a vacant parking slot in the line. There was only one person visible in the cab. "Okay, there's our mark," Frank said. "Hang tight."

The driver of the Kenworth refer drove the rig into the parking slot. Frank pulled the ATS tanker alongside the Kenworth's passenger side and waited to see what the driver was going to do next.

The guy shut the rig down and climbed from the cab. He started across the parking lot toward the truck-stop.

When he was in front of the ATS rig, Frank shouted at him. "Hey, buddy, you got just a second?"

The driver seemed surprised, but he stopped hesitantly. "What say?"

"I asked you if you got a second," Frank said again. He opened the cab door and climbed down. He met the guy on the ground in front of the ATS rig. "Howdy, name's Frankie. I wanted to know if you could answer a question for me. I'm sort of lost. I got this atlas over here and it doesn't tell me what I need to know. It's that or I don't know how to read the damned thing. Would you mind?"

"My name is Pete. Nice to meet you." He offered his hand and Frank accepted. "I get lost myself sometimes. Where's the atlas."

"Over here," Frank said. He turned and walked toward the ATS cab.

Pete followed.

They reached the cab. Frank climbed up and opened the door. He scrutinized the lot with a fast visual sweep to see if anyone was looking. He saw no one, so he sat in the driver's seat and lifted an old atlas from the console. "Here we are, Pete. Climb up and have a look."

Pete stepped up on the step and grabbed the

handrail beside the door. He leaned into the cab and looked at the atlas.

Frank's left arm swung out and locked around Pete's neck before the guy knew what had happened. Frank squeezed and twisted in the same motion. His right hand flew forward with his fingers tight against the palm. The heel near the wrist caught Pete on the tip of his nose. The chilling sound of bones breaking popped inside the cab. Frank crushed Pete's ethmoid bone and slammed the sharp edges deep into the guy's brain.

Blood flew and spurted from Pete's nose and mouth. He gasped and struggled for a split second, his eyes opened wide in horrified disbelief. Then his body jerked and trembled for a few seconds before it fell limp.

Frank tugged Pete onto the floorboard of the rig. He reached into the front pocket of the guy's jeans and found the keys to his rig. Then he glanced back at Dermont Ashland, who had watched the assault through the curtains of the sleeper. "Let's hit it, Mr. Ashland," Frank said.

Frank was out of the cab and on the ground before Ashland climbed completely through the sleeper curtains. Frank shoved Pete's feet onto the floor and left the man crumpled on the floorboard in a pool of blood.

Ashland cleared the door and climbed slowly and deliberately from the cab. When his feet hit the ground, Frank slammed the door closed and walked nonchalantly toward Pete's Kenworth. When they got to the cab of the big blue rig, Frank unlocked the door and climbed inside. He checked the sleeper to be sure a swapper wasn't asleep there. Satisfied that everything was clear, he jumped back to the ground and helped Dermont Ashland climb inside.

The old man made his way into the sleeper and Frank climbed into the driver's seat behind him. He inserted the proper key into the ignition and fired the diesel engine. He checked around the parking lot again to be sure no one was watching, then he dropped the rig into gear and headed for Ardmore, Alabama.

The Highway Warriors had run I-81 through Virginia to just outside of Knoxville, Tennessee. They switched drivers at Dandrige, Tennessee, and picked up I-40 westbound. Once they were through Knoxville, they had driven I-75 to Chattanooga and then cut across U.S. 74 to I-24. They ran west to the little town of South Pittsburg and headed south on U.S. 72 into Alabama. When U.S. 72 intersected with U.S. 231–431 near Normal, Alabama, Marc turned the rig south toward Huntsville and the horror that awaited them there.

Marc glanced over his shoulder and yelled to Carl, who was asleep in the sleeper. "Hey, Major, it's time to get up. We're almost in Huntsville."

Carl mumbled something unintelligible and finally stuck his head through the curtains. "Short naps kill me. I think I'd feel better if I didn't sleep at all."

Marc shot a glance over his shoulder. "You're a thing a beauty when you first wake up."

"Yeah, ain't I now?" Carl quipped. He rubbed his face with both hands and yawned. "What's new?"

"I talked to Brittin about an hour ago. They still haven't gotten Ashland and they can't find the senator. A field agent from the Bureau is going to meet us once we get in town and call Brittin on the link. We're going in under the guise of military intelligence. They'll give us some time with the woman scientist. Maybe she can shed more light on what is really going on in this town."

"How far we have to go?" Carl asked.

"I figure about ten more miles. If you're awake, you

can go ahead and make the call to Brittin. Get the agent en route to meet us."

Carl climbed into the front and settled in the passenger's seat. He lifted the Icom microphone from its cradle and made the call to Brittin Crain at FBI headquarters in Washington via the ComSat-D satellite link. "Barnburner, this is Pathfinder. Do you copy? Over."

The squelch tail sounded and Carl waited.

"Roger, Pathfinder, this is Barnburner. Over."

"Okay, Brittin, we're almost in Huntsville. Do you have directions for us to meet your man?"

Crain's voice crackled through the Icom speaker. "Affirmative. Stand by and I'll get the field people on the horn. Over."

"Roger," Carl said.

A few seconds passed and Crain's voice came across the speaker again. "Pathfinder, where are you now? Over."

Carl looked for a sign, found one, and gave the information to Crain. "We're on 231-431 southbound just north of Huntsville."

Several more seconds passed and Crain's voice rumbled from the Icom speaker. Crain recited the directions slowly so Carl would be sure to copy them correctly. "Roger, Pathfinder. The man in the field says that is Memorial Drive. Keep going south until you intersect with Governor's Drive. It's the second major cross street. It shouldn't be but a few more miles. Take a right on Governor's Drive and pull off on the shoulder. You won't be far from Marshall when you stop. The agent will meet you there. Over."

"You have an ETA?" Carl asked.

"Affirmative. Five to seven minutes. Is that a Roger?"

"Roger, Barnburner, we'll see your man there in five to seven. Pathfinder clear."

"Got it," Marc said. "Governor's Drive." He continued south on U.S. 231-431. The first major intersection appeared at University Drive. Marc sat in the afternoon traffic and waited for the four-way traffic light to turn green for traffic on Memorial Drive. "You know much about Redstone Arsenal, Major?" Marc asked.

"No, not much. I've heard about it somewhere in the past. You know much?"

"Some. I know it used to be the foremost chemical and biological research facility for the United States government. It was also a testing facility for development of the engines for most of the manned space flights for NASA. They did a good bit of work on the Saturn moon rockets as I understand it. At one time, the place had over twenty-five thousand employees. I think there are less than three or four thousand there today. Most of the people who still work there are employees of independent NASA contractors like Rockwell and Morton Thiocol. Today, all of the space-shuttle engines are test-fired at Marshall before they are actually used on a shuttle. Marshall is also the primary developer for America's manned space station. The R-and-D mock-up is being built there. I've heard the place is like a ghost town since the cutbacks by NASA and the military. There are acres and acres of unused buildings. Sad in a way. What was once a nerve center for man's conquest of outer space is now just a redundant control center for routine shuttle missions. Amazing how the climate changes, huh?"

"Yeah," Carl said.

The light turned green and Marc eased the rig forward. They traveled across the intersection and up a slight grade on Memorial Drive. In a few minutes,

Governor's Drive appeared. Marc coasted the high-tech Leeco machine toward the intersection and made a turn to the right. He found a vacant spot on the shoulder of the road and parked.

Two minutes passed and a brown Pontiac appeared. The driver pulled the car in front of the Leeco rig and parked. A tall young man wearing a jogging suit got out and walked toward the cab.

Marc opened his door and climbed out.

The man in the jogging suit stopped at the driver's door of the Leeco cab and stared at Marc. "Good afternoon. Are you Colonel Lee or Major Browne by chance?"

"I'm Colonel Lee and that's Major Browne in the cab," Marc said.

"Great. I'm Special Agent Dennis Hargrove." he offered a handshake and Marc accepted. "My office said you'd be in a truck. This machine caught me off guard. I thought they meant a pickup or a Bronco, something like that. I guess when they said a truck, they meant a *truck*. If you'll follow me, I'll take you to our office. Dr. Caldwell will be there."

"Before we go," Marc said, "do you think this woman is on the level? Is there really a laboratory underground around here?"

"Colonel," Hargrove said, "people don't come running to the FBI wearing a nightgown with a tale as bizarre as this one. This lady is extremely intelligent. She's scared out of her mind and her credentials check out. To answer your question . . . I believe every word she's said."

"Okay," Marc said. "You lead the way."

Hargrove nodded, turned, and walked toward his car.

Marc climbed back aboard the Leeco rig and waited

for Hargrove to move out. They merged into the light traffic and drove for five minutes until they reached a small strip of offices. Hargrove parked and waited for the Highway Warriors to climb from the rig.

They met in the parking lot.

"Agent Hargrove, this is Major Browne," Marc said. He gestured toward Carl.

"Pleased to meet you, Major," Hargrove replied.

"Same here," Carl said, and he and Hargrove shook hands.

"This way," Hargrove said. He led the way to a suite of offices in the corner of the L-shaped strip. "As I told you, Colonel, this woman is scared out of her mind. Go as easy on her as you can."

"Understood," Marc replied.

They entered the offices and walked straight to a conference room in the rear of the complex. Hargrove knocked on a door and then entered without waiting for a reply.

Dr. Caldwell was seated at the end of a long conference table. She looked frayed and weary. She was wrapped in a green government-issue wool blanket.

"Dr. Caldwell," Hargrove said. "This is Colonel Lee and Major Browne from army intelligence. They would like to talk with you. Are you amenable to that?"

Caldwell looked at Marc and Carl. She sat silent for a long moment, her eyes locked with theirs. "Yes, I'll talk with them. I'll do anything to stop the horror those people are ready to unleash. They must be stopped or the lives of millions of people are in serious jeopardy."

"Dr. Caldwell," Marc said. "Tell us what you know about this facility and what has taken place there. We need all of the details you can recall if we are to make a significant effort at curtailing this problem."

"I can tell you everything there is to know about the

facility and the people in there. There is only one thing I don't know. I don't know who they are or where they came from. They are murderers and they kill without conscience. Many of my colleagues are dead; maybe all of them by now. It must be stopped."

"Okay," Marc said. "Start at the beginning. If we have questions, we'll stop you. Is that all right?"

Dr. Caldwell spent ten minutes replaying the scenario the same way she had with the FBI agents when she had first arrived at their offices. She recited elaborate details of the events that had occurred in the middle of the night at the facility. When she was finished, she looked at the Highway Warriors. "That's about it," she said.

"Would you be willing to take us to this place?" Marc asked.

Caldwell was hesitant at first. "I don't know if I can go back there. I'm sorry."

"Is there any way we can get into the lab without being detected?" Carl asked.

"There are only two ways in. One is the elevator, and the other is through the escape tunnel I used to get out. There is still a problem with that."

"The chemical gases in the containment unit," Marc said.

"Exactly. If you breathe those chemicals, you'd be dead in a matter of seconds. Even with the time that has elapsed since I released them, they are still quite potent," Caldwell said.

"So it's the front door or no way at all?" Carl asked.

"Yes. Well, wait a minute. Maybe not. I left the suit in the underbrush. It might fit you, Colonel Lee, but I know it's too small for Major Browne. Even for you, it would be a snug fit. I think you could make it, though."

"So if I had the suit, I could get inside and gain

entrance to the main compound without detection. Is that correct?" Marc asked.

Caldwell was momentarily reluctant to answer. "Yes, if you follow my exact instructions, then maybe you would have a decent chance at success. There would be no margin for error. If you make a mistake, it would cost you your life. If you made the right mistake once you're inside the unit, it could kill everyone inside there."

"Is it possible to handle a weapon while wearing the suit?" Marc asked.

"No," Caldwell said flatly. "The glove section is much too cumbersome. These suits are made for handling large metal canisters. They weren't designed for delicate work. We have others that would be usable, but they're in another section of the lab. And there is one thing I just thought of."

"What's that?" Marc asked.

"The chute with the ladder that leads from ground level to the tunnel below is straight down. It's a long, narrow hole. If you slip on that ladder or someone is below and they hear you coming, there is nowhere for you to go. You must move up or down. If you fail, you're unquestionably dead."

"My, you're encouraging," Carl said.

"I want you to know what you're getting into if you try to enter through the tunnel. That laboratory has become a hellhole."

Marc smiled. "Dr. Caldwell, I've spent more than half of my life in hellholes. I do my best work there."

Dr. Caldwell was flabbergasted. She sat erect and stared at the Highway Warriors.

"He's right," Carl said. "What's hell to you is home to us. This is the kind of thing the colonel and I are best at. It's what we are trained for."

Caldwell was silent. She sat that way for a long

moment before she spoke. "There are at least twelve of them in there. Only one of you can go in. You'll be drastically outnumbered. Also, you mustn't negate the presence of Dr. von Wirth. If he is involved in this, as I suspect he is, then he can be a very dangerous man."

"Thanks for the warning," Marc said.

A knock sounded at the door and a young secretary stuck her head inside. "Agent Hargrove, I have an urgent telephone call for you. Line five."

Hargrove jumped to his feet. "Would you please excuse me." He left the room and closed the door behind him.

Marc looked at Carl. "Radio communications will be useless inside the lab. When I go in, I'm on my own. Unless something changes, you cover the top entrance at the old barn Dr. Caldwell mentioned. If anything comes out, take it down and ask questions later."

"I think we need to use two different vehicles. I can go in using the rig. You and Dr. Caldwell can use one of the Cherokees," Carl said.

"I agree," Marc said. "That way, if something breaks, one of us won't be stranded." He looked at Caldwell. "Is there any idea about what happened to the elevator?"

"Something happened when the tremor rocked through the facility. I don't know what it was," Caldwell said.

"Is it possible the insurgents have repaired it?" Carl asked.

"Anything is possible. If anyone down there has found the way to defeat the airlocks, then yes, it is possible."

"What if they're already out, Colonel?" Carl asked.

"Then we have a major problem," Marc replied.

"Yeah, that brings us to another major problem.

Don't forget we have that contraption that everybody seemed so damned concerned about. One of us is gonna have to hold that thing in safekeeping."

"I figure if you're with the rig, then the gizmo is safe. You agree?"

"I could make the delivery on the way to the lab. What about that?" Carl asked.

"Check with the general on the way over to Marshall and see what he says," Marc said.

The door opened and Agent Hargrove walked in. "I've got a problem, gentlemen and lady. I need to be with you guys at Marshall, but three agents have located Dermont Ashland and Frank Montino. They have them under observation at a warehouse in Ardmore. I think we need to take them down before I get involved in a move on the laboratory. If those people are trapped belowground, they aren't going anywhere. I can't say the same for Ashland and Montino."

"You want some help?" Carl asked.

"I don't see why not. All of this seems to be related. These men have killed six federal agents. One more gun might come in handy."

"Okay," Marc said. "Let's get one of the jeeps off-loaded and Dr. Caldwell and I can go to the lab. Carl, you go with Agent Hargrove to Ardmore. If you can take Ashland alive, maybe we can find out what is really going down here."

Dr. Caldwell looked at the men, her face was etched with serious concern. "Let me say this one more time, gentlemen. If those canisters get out of the laboratory and their contents get into the atmosphere, millions of people will die. We cannot permit that to happen."

Marc smiled at Dr. Caldwell. "If Jon and his companions are still in that facility when I get there, they won't be going anywhere. When we get in the vehicles, switch your radio to F-fourteen-simplex. I have a plan and I think we can stop this horror in Huntsville before it spreads like one of those bacteriological plagues."

# Chapter Fifteen

□ □ □

"Nadimi," Jon yelled. "How much longer?"

"Soon, my brother. We have removed ten of the canisters to the top now. We are waiting to load them on the truck." Nadimi was out of breath. He moved quickly, and the pause to speak to Jon was a relief.

"Very good. And the elevator, it is working all right?"

"Yes," Nadimi said. "We have made two trips to the top. There was a slight problem with the third airlock from the top. The security code had to be bypassed. We have corrected the problem now and I think all will go well."

"Good, when the last of the cargo is taken to the top, bring the hostages back to the lab. I also want one large explosive charge. I have a nice surprise in store for them."

"You are going to blow up the laboratory? Isn't that dangerous?"

"Not all of it. I only want to detonate one special area. It is the least I can do to repay young Dr. Caldwell for her hospitality."

"Very well, Jon. I must get on about my business now," Nadimi said.

"Yes, Nadimi, carry on with the work of our brotherhood." Jon smiled and patted Nadimi on the back. "You are a good and dedicated man, Nadimi. I wish I could have more men with your fortitude. My work would be easier."

"Thank you, Jon," Nadimi said. "I must go."

"Yes," Jon said. "You must."

Nadimi left with three other insurgents and three hostages. They walked quickly to Containment Unit 2 in the rear of the laboratory. Each hostage took a sealed canister and carried it into the hallway. Nadimi watched every move the hostages made. One by one, they lifted the heavy canisters and moved slowly toward the front of the facility and the elevator.

At the front, Jon was with Dr. von Wirth. He watched the old man while the hostages loaded chemical weapons into the elevator. "Doctor, it will be time for us to go soon. Is there anything you wish to take with you? If there is, I can have one of my men gather it."

"Thank you, Jon," von Wirth said. "I have some files and personal notebooks I would like to take. Interesting, isn't it?"

"What's that, doctor?" Jon asked.

"Interesting that an entire lifetime can be reduced to a small stack of notebooks with formulas, methods, and ideas. When I was a young man, I thought there would be so much more to one's life than this. So very much more. It amazes me that youth possesses the ability to deceive the rational mind so cleverly. Until you're old, you hardly realize it has occurred."

Jon didn't know what to say. He looked puzzled and almost irritated. "Where are these things, doctor? I will have one of my men care for them for you."

Von Wirth pointed to a small white cabinet across

the room. "In there, Jon. My entire lifetime is in that white cabinet."

Jon looked into the hallway and saw Nadimi. He called to him. "Nadimi, come here please."

"Yes, Jon?" Nadimi asked when he stopped at the doorway.

"Nadimi, have one of the men come in here and remove the contents of that small white cabinet." He pointed to it across the room. "Have the contents transported with us for Dr. von Wirth. See that they are cared for impeccably."

"Yes, sir. It is done."

Nadimi called to one of the insurgents in the area near the elevator. He relayed the message and the insurgent complied. He removed the contents and placed them in a corrugated box to be transported to the surface with the next load of canisters.

The elevator doors opened and the insurgents instructed the hostages to load the third load of deadly materials for the trip to the surface. It took three minutes to move the heavy canisters into the large freight-size elevator.

Nadimi waved to the insurgents, giving them the go-ahead to take the load to the surface. "See if you can find our recon man when you get up there. We must know the status of the other teams," he said just as the door was closing.

One of the insurgents nodded his head to indicate that he understood.

The doors closed and the elevator moved slowly toward the surface and the awaiting eighteen-wheelers that would carry the chemical and bacteriological weapons to a new location.

Nadimi walked away from the doors toward the rear of the facility. He decided to go to Containment Unit 2 and make a quick count of the remaining canisters. He was near the door that led into the hallway when a thunderous rumble roared through the elevator shaft. A hurricanelike burst of scorching wind shot through the shaft. When it reached the bottom, the force blew the doors from their mounts and sent lethal shards of metallic shrapnel flying through the room with deadly velocity.

The shrapnel cut into Nadimi's flesh and shredded him like a thousand angry piranhas attacking at once. He fell to the floor and gasped for breath, but the intensity of the chemical compounds now present in the air made breathing impossible. He gasped hard and choked, but there was no escape from the deadly vapors. In one final and gallant surge of loyalty to his cause, he managed to get to his knees and hit the airtight door. It slammed closed and secured the area, effectively locking most of the deadly chemicals in the reception area of the facility. He collapsed back toward the floor and his fingernails scraped the paint from the back side of the door as he fell. His eyes were opened wide in sheer horror as blood trickled from his mouth and ears. With life gone from him, he rested in a pool of blood on the floor.

Jon was on his feet and running at the first sound and vibration of the explosion. He reached the outer door an instant after it slammed closed. He hit it with his shoulder, but it wouldn't open. Dennis and three other insurgents joined him while Dr. von Wirth stood watching without emotion. Jon turned toward von Wirth, fear etched across his face and his eyes disclosing the horror ravaging him. "We're trapped, aren't we?"

Von Wirth still displayed no emotion. "Yes, it would appear that way. Perhaps 'entombed' is a better word, Jon. It is not the entrapment that is our most important concern. What we should fear is the compound or compounds that entered our ventilation system from that explosion. And for the sake of those on the surface, pray that the upper airlocks contained the residue, lest we have done a grave injustice to mankind."

A hard and forceful voice blared over a public-address system. "Dermont Ashland. Frank Montino. This is the FBI. The building you are occupying is surrounded. You have thirty seconds to throw out your weapons and come out of the building with your hands over your head. If you do not comply immediately, we will use deadly force to effect your capture."

"Holy shit! How did they find us this time?" Frank yelled.

"What do we do, Frank, surrender?"

"Not in this lifetime," Frank replied. "Get in the truck. We're going out of here."

"Frank, we can't outrun them. They'll find us again."

"Okay, you want to surrender, you surrender. I'm haulin' ass." Frank climbed aboard the stolen Kenworth and fired the diesel engine.

Dermont Ashland knew he was faced with perhaps the most critical decision of his lifetime. And he knew if he made the wrong choice, it could very well be the last decision also.

He climbed aboard the rig.

Frank floored the engine and popped the clutch. The big rig burst to life and crashed through the huge warehouse door. Wood and debris flew in every direction when the rig penetrated the door. Frank grabbed another gear and cut hard right toward the highway as he careened across the warehouse lot.

Gunfire erupted and bullets slapped into the safety glass of the Kenworth's windshield.

Ashland ducked and screamed in the same motion.

Frank fought for control as the big eighteen-wheeler crashed into a dark car with two men crouched behind it. The men scattered and ran an instant before the speeding Kenworth's bumper slammed it backward. The rig rocked onto the highway as Frank grabbed another gear.

Carl sat patiently in the Leeco rig across the highway beside a volunteer fire station and watched as the Kenworth made its getaway attempt. When the Kenworth rolled onto the highway, he kicked the Leeco machine into gear. He picked up his Icom handheld and made a short call. "Hargrove, you boys just lay back. The sucka's mine now. I'll take him down."

"You got it," Hargrove replied. "We don't have the equipment to fight him, but we'll back you up."

"Affirmative," Carl replied. He laid the handheld radio on the console and grabbed another gear. Then he reached to the computer console and moved the appropriate switches to activate the rig's weapons systems. For the sake of safety, he switched on the CAS and the ODS. That done, he armed the front-mounted Stinger miniguns and the 20mm cannons recessed into the front bumper and grille.

Montino was pushing the Kenworth hard. Spurting streams of black smoke shot from the smokestacks along both sides of the rig. They reached the traffic light at the railroad underpass on the Alabama–Tennessee state line. Montino didn't wait for the light to change. He plowed through the line of stopped traffic and knocked a half-dozen cars off the road as he sideswiped them while attempting to pass on the left side of the narrow two-lane road. He cleared the intersection, passed under the railroad, and crossed the line into Tennessee.

Carl was right behind him. He threaded his way

through the wreckage at the intersection and hit another gear. The massive custom diesel engine in the Leeco machine roared thunder as Carl pushed to catch the speeding Kenworth.

They were on the outskirts of the little town of Ardmore when Carl finally gained enough ground to close on the fleeing rig. He picked up the handheld and yelled at Hargrove. "He's making a run for the interstate. I'm going to take him down as soon as he clears the populated areas. Don't get too close because if he doesn't stop, there'll likely be one hell of a fire in front of me."

"Roger," Hargrove replied. "We're behind you, but we'll hold about a hundred yards off your tail. Is that ten-four?"

"Ten-four," Carl replied, and tossed the Icom into the passenger seat.

Montino was running hard in the Kenworth. He gained speed and dodged vehicles on the highway. Carl was less than fifty feet off the end of his trailer when suddenly the brake lights came on and the giant rig swerved.

Carl braked hard and ignored the warning from the ODS and CAS. He swerved also, the Leeco machine going right and onto the shoulder.

Montino cut to the left and clipped the front end of a pickup truck preparing for a left turn.

The Kenworth rolled across the oncoming lane and crashed through a row of hedges in front of a Hardee's drive-thru restaurant. Montino cut back onto the highway without slowing down.

"Jesus, Frank, you're going to get us killed," Ashland bellowed.

"Stay calm, Mr. Ashland. It ain't over yet." He grabbed another gear and the Kenworth's engine whined.

Carl cleared the wreckage of the pickup and moved back onto the regularly traveled portion of the highway. He shoved the clutch in and grabbed another gear to try to regain his lost speed. He was closing fast again now, the Leeco machine less than a hundred feet from the back of the Kenworth's trailer.

Montino drove hard. He clipped the rear of a pickup truck hauling a load of hay. The truck spun around two or three times on the side of the highway and loose hay flew wildly in every direction.

Carl closed the gap. They were out of town now and the residences that had lined the highway were gone. There were houses visible, but most of them sat off the roadway a safe distance. He moved to the tailgate of the Kenworth and slipped just over the center line of the highway with the left front tire of the custom machine.

Montino saw him and cut left. An oncoming car swerved completely off the road and into a cornfield to avoid a collision.

Carl cut back into the proper lane and moved in to nudge the rear of the trailer.

Montino slammed on his brakes.

The CAS beeped an ear-piercing warning and the Leeco rig braked down with its antilocking brakes to avoid the collision. When the Kenworth moved forward and the Leeco rig was out of danger, the CAS released and Carl hit the accelerator hard again. He moved on tight to the tail of the trailer, adjusted his speed, and hugged tightly to the fleeing rig. He reached over to the armaments control and lifted it to his lap. He realized he couldn't drive and watch the computer screen for the electronic sight at the same time. He kept his eyes on the road and the Kenworth while he reached behind the seat and found the optical sight helmet. He pulled it to his lap, unwound the connecting cable, and slipped the twenty-five-pin plug into the computer's front-bay serial port. He slid the helmet over his head with his right hand while he steered with his left. When it felt in place, he pressed the activation switch, dropped the hood, and he was ready for battle. The Kenworth and everything on the highway appeared on a small optical screen over his left eye. He could see the target sight, system status, and armament selection through the screen. He could also see the highway just as clearly as if the helmet was not in place. "Damn, I love this technology," he mumbled aloud.

They reached a long straightaway and Montino pushed the Kenworth for all it was worth. The rigs rolled over the narrow road at dangerously high speed. Carl glanced at the digital speedometer on the console of the high-tech Leeco machine. It read 114 miles per hour.

Carl aligned the electronic sight and touched his finger to the firing mechanism when the Stinger miniguns homed in on the rear of the Kenworth's trailer. He started squeezing the firing switch when a line of four cars appeared in the oncoming lane. He changed his mind, released pressure on the switch.

Both rigs shot by the oncoming cars and started down a winding grade toward the bottom of a hill. Montino had the giant Kenworth struggling to stay on the paved portion of the highway. Carl waited for a chance to fire, but he couldn't get a clear view of what was ahead.

He waited.

The rigs bottomed out on the winding grade and started up the other side of the hill. Carl glanced ahead now and he could see the interchange for I-65.

He pressed the accelerator further toward the floor and closed hard on the bandit rig. When they topped the hill at the interstate highway, Montino cut left.

The Kenworth leaned and left a trail of black marks and rubber smoke when Montino negotiated the ninety-degree turn onto the entry ramp to I-65 south.

Carl slowed the Leeco machine and negotiated the turn. He glanced down onto the interstate to see how traffic was flowing.

It was light.

He pressed the pedal to the floor and rolled through the gears. The Leeco rig gained speed again and moved down the ramp with diesel smoke pouring from its gleaming chrome stacks. The massive custom engine sent brute-force torque to the transmission and drive-shaft.

The Kenworth was on the interstate now. A two-ton stake truck had swerved to the left to avoid hitting the stolen rig when it forced its way onto the highway.

Carl slowed for a second, dodged the out-of-control two-by, and straightened the rig on the interstate headed south.

Montino cut in and out of traffic as he fought to maintain control and tried desperately to make his escape clean.

Carl weaved through the sparse traffic. He glanced in his rearview mirrors and saw Hargrove and two other agents holding steady a hundred yards back. He made his move to gain on the Kenworth.

Montino saw him coming. He sideswiped a four-wheeler and sent the little car into the median. The driver of the four-wheeler wasn't sure what had happened. He lost control, hit a drainage culvert, and flipped into the air. He crashed down on his top and rested snugly in the bottom of the median.

Carl tried the sight once more. He leveled the Stinger miniguns on the rear of the Kenworth, but the margin of safety for passersby was far too narrow to chance a burst of machine-gun fire. He took a deep breath and waited.

The rigs crossed back into Alabama south of the Ardmore exit. To the right, the nose cone of a rocket became visible. Carl glanced at it as the rigs sped past the rest area and Alabama welcome center. The gleaming white and black rocket sat on display at the welcome center and towered over everything in the area.

Carl looked back at the speeding Kenworth. Montino was in the left lane now and trying to overtake a southbound gasoline tanker. Carl watched closely and held his breath. If Montino sideswiped or collided with the tanker, it could all be over.

He didn't.

The rear of the Kenworth rig cleared the tanker and Montino cut back into the right lane. Ahead now, traffic thinned. Carl moved in for the kill. He caught the tanker and whizzed past it. The startled driver shot a mean look toward the Leeco machine when Carl overtook him.

The Kenworth was in the clear now. Traffic had dwindled to a point of safety. Carl moved in closer. He was off the tail of the Kenworth by less than fifty yards. He lined the electronic sight up on the rear of the trailer and fingered a burst of Stinger machine-gun rounds. The Leeco rig rumbled when the burst of hot lead left the machine like a swarm of angry hornets.

The rounds pelted into the rear or the trailer and penetrated the aluminum skin.

Montino initiated evasive action. He swerved the rig across both southbound lanes in an erratic zigzag pattern. Ahead now, there were two four-wheelers. Neither driver apparently saw the Kenworth coming. Montino was on them before their brake lights came on.

Carl slowed the Leeco rig.

Montino hit the first four-wheeler and sent him

spinning toward the shoulder of the highway. The driver lost control and the car disappeared over a small embankment.

The second driver saw the Kenworth now, but it was far too late. Montino slammed into the beige Nissan and knocked it from the roadway. The car became airborne and landed nose-first into the median. Then it tumbled over and over before it finally came to rest on its side.

Carl closed the narrowing gap. He aligned the sight and fingered the automatic tracking function on the computer. The electronic sight moved with the snakelike flow of the Kenworth. Carl touched the firing button and another burst of sizzling hornets belched from the bores of the machine guns. The sizzlers riveted the rear of the trailer, but Montino didn't slow.

The Kenworth chewed more pavement and kept up the zigzag pattern from side to side of the southbound highway.

Carl closed the gap further. He was almost even with the tail of the trailer now. He opened the helmet-mounted microphone for the public-address system. His voice blared across the Alabama countryside with 250 watts of audio intensity. "Montino, give it up. I'm gonna get serious back here if you don't stop. You have no route of escape. Pull the rig to the shoulder and surrender now."

Montino ignored the order, but inside the cab Dermont Ashland was pale from the highest level of fear he had ever known in his life. "Maybe we better stop, Frank."

"No way," Frank shouted. "He wants me, he'll have to kill me. That's the only way I'll ever stop."

Carl moved in and fired another burst of machine-gun fire that strafed along the left side of the Kenworth. Small pieces of metal flew, but the rig didn't stop.

He fingered still another burst and this time the inside right rear tire exploded. Huge pieces of black rubber became airborne from the rolling velocity of the Kenworth. Carl swerved to avoid a big section of the disintegrated tire.

Carl moved back in on the tail of the Kenworth trailer again. He followed the zigzag pattern initiated by Montino and both rigs snaked back and forth across the highway.

Carl almost touched the rear of the Kenworth with the front bumper of the Leeco rig.

Montino slammed on his brakes and the Kenworth swerved crazily across the highway.

Carl had no place to go except past the bandit rig. He floored the accelerator and shot ahead of Montino and Ashland. He changed the sight tracking to the rear of the custom war machine and watched Montino in the rearview mirrors. Then he had a plan.

Carl punched the powerplant throttle and the Leeco machine sped ahead. He picked up the Icom. "Hargrove, shut off all traffic on the highway. Block it and stand by until I call you again. Don't let anything get past you."

"What's up?" Hargrove asked.

"Just hang on and don't let that traffic get past," Carl replied.

Carl maintained high speed until he was a mile ahead of Montino and Ashland in the Kenworth. He mentally assessed the terrain, and as he rounded a winding curve on a downgrade, he made the decision. He braked hard on the rig and rolled toward the right shoulder. He mentally aligned his necessary path and positioned the rig with the rear end near the center of the highway and the cab approaching the shoulder. The angle appeared perfect.

He activated the high-definition television and the video recorder. He quickly checked the status of the rear weapons and opened the cannon and rocket ports.

Montino rounded the curve and saw the rig cross-ways the highway. He hit his brakes briefly and then floored the pedal.

"You shoulda listened, assholes," Carl bellowed, and touched the firing mechanism. A rumble thudded through the Leeco machine. A whoosh followed the heavy chatter of automatic cannon fire. A pair of deadly heat-seeking, infrared guided rockets flew toward the front of the Kenworth.

Dermont Ashland saw it an instant before impact. He screamed in undiluted horror. "No!" But his last scream was swallowed by the intense explosion and his final facial expression was melted away by unforgiving cleansing fire.

Frank Montino saw it also. His eyes opened wide and he took a deep breath, but all his lungs could inhale was fire and smoke. Even before the combination could suffocate him, he was dead.

The flaming Kenworth careened out of control and plummeted over the embankment on the left shoulder of the highway. The diesel fuel tanks ruptured and high-grade kerosene fueled the already intense fire. The rig came to rest in a mass of fire-engulfed twisted metal.

Carl picked up the Icom. "Hargrove, you can take these two off of your most-wanted list. I'm on my way to Marshall to help the colonel."

# Chapter Sixteen

□ □ □

Marc crouched low in the underbrush. Dr. Kathleen Caldwell crouched beside him. She was dressed in jeans and a flannel shirt donated by one of the secretaries at the FBI office. They moved slowly to the place where she had hidden the protective pressurized suit.

They had driven the Jeep Cherokee to within a hundred yards of their current position. There had been no road there, but Marc had dropped into four-wheel drive and plowed through the low-lying underbrush with ease.

Dr. Caldwell pointed to an area twenty yards from where she and Marc hid. "The suit is over there. I don't think you'll see it until we're right on top of it."

"Lead the way," Marc said.

Caldwell moved stealthily through the brush. She got to the place where she had stashed the suit and she stopped. She dropped to her knees and started digging. In seconds, the off-white suit became visible. "Here we are. Just like I left it."

"Fantastic," Marc said. He knelt and helped Caldwell uncover the protective suit.

They lifted the heavy apparatus from the ground and beat the outside with their hands to rid it of loose dirt and leaf particles. Caldwell held it up against Marc's shoulders. "It will be tight, but I think you can wear it. You may find it uncomfortable at first, but given a few minutes, you'll get used to it."

"It beats the alternative. Chemical poisoning isn't my idea of a good time," Marc said. He laid his sound-suppressed Uzi on the ground and started climbing into the suit.

Caldwell helped and secured all of the necessary hardware. She activated the pressure unit on the backpack and checked the gauges. "Okay," she said, "you're ready."

Marc spoke through the helmet-mounted audio amplifier. "These things certainly weren't built for comfort, were they?"

"No," Caldwell replied. "They were designed for the ultimate in environmental protection. There are some larger sizes in the decontamination unit, but if you follow my previous instructions to the letter, you won't need it. If you don't do exactly as I told you, you won't need either one of them."

"You're an encouraging young woman, doctor," Marc replied.

"And you are a daring young man, Colonel. Be careful down there."

Marc smiled through the helmet face piece. "Would you harness all of my accessories onto the rings here?"

Caldwell nodded. "Sure. Remember, if you don't find any of the lab personnel alive, get out of there. Use the atmospheric-quality measuring device I told you about. It's in the decontamination unit. It will give you an accurate reading of the air quality. If it shows anything over point three, don't take the suit off. If you do, you won't come out of that hole."

Marc checked his weapons and accessories. He

carried the Uzi strapped to a snap D-ring on the front of the suit. His musette bag was snapped to the left side of the suit on another D-ring. He slung his nylon web belt and holster with all of the accessories for the Smith & Wesson 5906 across his right shoulder. He carried a coil of climbing rope and several rubber cargo straps for emergency use.

"That does it," Marc said. "Now it's your turn to remember something. If I'm not out of that hole in forty-five minutes, it means I'm probably not coming out. In that case, you know what to do. I don't want any hesitation either. Just do it and be done with it all."

Caldwell's face showed signs of emotion when a tear developed in one corner of her eye. "Are you sure?"

Marc's voice turned instantly firm. "Doctor, I'm absolutely positive. We can't chance the possibility of a leak that would contaminate half of civilization for the sake of a handful of people. Any way you slice it, it isn't worth it."

Caldwell nodded hesitant agreement.

The Icom handheld radio on her belt crackled with Carl's voice. "You there, Colonel? Over."

"Would you hold that up here for me, doctor?" Marc asked.

Caldwell held the radio to the front of the helmet and pressed the push-to-talk switch. "Go ahead, Major."

"I'm on my way to Marshall. Ashland and Montino didn't see things my way. They learned a lesson about cleansing hellfire. Both of 'em are toast. Over."

"Affirmative," Marc said. "I'm going in the hole. Locate the doctor when you get here. Over."

"Affirmative," Carl replied. "Be careful. For your information, I see a convoy of about a dozen concrete trucks moving east on Governor's Drive."

"Roger that. See you when I see you."

"Roger," Carl replied.

Dr. Caldwell removed the handheld and placed it back on the belt of her jeans. "Good luck. I'll be waiting for you right here."

"Somehow, that makes it worth the effort," Marc said, and he smiled.

Caldwell returned the smile and hugged Marc through the heavy pressurized suit.

Marc moved low in a crouch toward the entrance to the chute that would take him far belowground into the tunnel and eventually into the underground laboratory. He reached the concealed hatch, opened it, and took a long hard look at the dark hole below. Without hesitation, he climbed onto the first rungs of the ladder and descended below ground level. Once he was inside he closed the hatch behind him, but left it unsecured. The hole became as dark as pitch with only the dull glow of a dim light at the bottom of the cylindrical shaft.

Marc moved slowly and deliberately in the darkness. He checked every step before he took it to ensure that his footing was correct and stable. He stopped every ten or twelve steps and listened, but the only sound he heard was his own rhythmic breathing echoing through the shaft.

The descent took fifteen minutes, but Marc finally saw the intensity of the dull light increase. He was ten steps from the tunnel and he decided to stop and listen again.

There was still only the sound of his own breath going in and coming out.

He finished the descent into the tunnel. Marc stopped and evaluated the instructions given him by Dr. Caldwell. He made a mental checklist, then he checked his accessories and moved toward the closed hatch at the back of Containment Unit 1.

There was no sound from inside the facility. It caused Marc to wonder if the insurgents had escaped before he arrive or if, by some quirk, everyone inside was already dead. He let the thought go and went to work on the security latch that held the airlock door closed from the tunnel side.

The latch opened easily and Marc pulled gently on the door until the sound of the airlock breaking its seal filled the tunnel. He peeped inside. Nothing moved and he heard nothing. He felt his heart rate increase and his breathing quickened.

Marc opened the door far enough to crawl through and he went inside.

First things first.

Marc closed the door behind him and quickly found the control panel on the back wall exactly where Dr. Caldwell had told him it would be. He found the color-coded switches and moved them.

A muffled sound rumbled throughout the containment unit and the tunnel. The auxiliary air ventilation system kicked in. That system would purge the air going inside the tunnel of any chemical residue that might have leaked when the door to the containment unit was compromised. It would also clear the air inside the containment unit itself, and Marc knew he would need that before his mission was accomplished. That was, if anyone was still alive inside.

Marc fumbled with his musette bag and managed to get two Delta Force Compound-Two explosive units out. He fixed them in place for future use and set the timers for twenty-five minutes on the LCD display attached to each one. That finished, he moved around the aisles of assorted death canisters and found three that had been identified by Dr. Caldwell. He lifted them from the shelves and placed them near the doorway at the back wall.

Marc carefully checked to be sure there was no one in the hallway outside of the containment unit. He neither saw nor heard anyone and that made him feel uneasy.

He moved toward the front and the narrow steel stairway that led into the overhead tunnel to Decontamination Unit 1. He walked quickly and climbed the stairs until he was out of sight from anyone who might happen through the hallway. It took only seconds and he was outside of the decontamination unit. He worked the security bar on the door and triggered the outer airlock release.

The seal on the door unseized. Marc opened it and entered the decontamination unit. He found the instrument Dr. Caldwell had told him to find. He switched it on with some difficulty and read the LED display. It showed .079. That meant the air was pure enough to breathe and free of chemical or bacteriological residue. It also meant he could rid himself of the cumbersome suit.

He did that quickly. He arranged his accessories and weapons the way he liked them and proceeded to the security seal on the outer door leading into the hallway. He reached it and made short work of the process. Like the others before, the airlock unseized and Marc was ready to move into the main facility.

He checked the Uzi, his Smith & Wesson 5906, and the Beretta 92-F. He also carried six hand grenades and six smoke grenades. There was an assortment of flash-bang compositions in his musette bag and spare sticks for each of the weapons. He checked the chamber in each of the firearms and slipped the hammer drops off on the Smith and the Beretta. If he needed either of the weapons in a hurry, there would be no time to think about moving them. The hammer-down position was a safe carry nonetheless. As a matter of habit, he checked the sound suppressor on the Uzi to be sure it was still tightly threaded. It was.

Marc glanced down at his wristwatch. He tapped the chronograph timer and opened the door into the hallway.

Showtime.

He moved slowly, the Uzi sweeping each section of hallway that appeared in front of him. He reached an intersection and a required turn that would take him to the residential section of the facility. He stopped and eased his head around the corner.

He jerked back. A man with an assault rifle stood poised in the hallway thirty feet away. The man walked up and down a short stretch of the hallway.

Marc waited, mentally tracking the guy's movements. When he thought he had the pattern down, Marc rolled into the hallway on his stomach with the Uzi ready to spit hellfire and death.

The armed guard turned, his assault rifle looking for a target.

Marc unleashed a three-round burst from the silenced subgun. The shooter twitched for a few seconds and spiraled to the floor.

Marc was on his feet and running toward the fallen insurgent before the guy even hit the floor. He grabbed the assault rifle from the man's dead hand, buttoned down the magazine, and ejected the live round from the chamber. Then he tossed the weapon across the hallway. He moved fast and checked each room with a doorway into the hall. When he reached the room in the center of the hall, he kicked the door open and rolled inside. Seven startled faces looked back at him . . . technicians and lab personnel. "Who are you people?" Marc asked.

One man spoke up. "We work here, or at least we did."

"I've come to get you out of here. How many others are there?"

"Us or them?" the man asked.

"Both," Marc replied.

"I only know of two more lab people. They killed everybody else. There must be eight or ten of them. Some of their people were killed when the elevator exploded about an hour ago. We lost three people there also. Who the hell are you?" the guy asked.

"Delta Force. Let it go at that," Marc replied. He glanced over his shoulder and then checked the hallway. Everything was still clear.

"How many of you people are there?" the guy asked.

Marc smiled. "You're looking at the rescue team. Let's go. You must do exactly as I say and I'll get you out of here. No arguments and no discussion. It's my way. Understand?"

Everyone nodded.

"Good. Where are the other two?"

"In the front near Dr. von Wirth's office. It will be the third door from this end of the hallway on the other end of the facility."

"And the insurgents. Where are they?"

"Last time we saw them, Jon, that's the leader, and five or six men were in von Wirth's office with the doctor."

Marc checked the hallway again. "All right, let's do it. Go directly to the decontamination unit across from Containment Unit One. Get inside there and take the tunnel into the containment unit. I'm right behind you."

A woman spoke up. "Containment Unit One is contaminated with chemical gases. We'll all die."

"Not anymore," Marc said. "I've cleared it. When you get inside, go straight to the back behind the aisles. Take the small airlock door. Crawl through it and go left in the tunnel. There is a ladder at the end. Get on and climb until you see daylight. People will be waiting for you there. Now get a move on!"

The hostages stood and moved to the door behind Marc. He jumped into the hallway and covered both ends as best he could. The hostages moved down the hallway and made the left turn to take them to the decontamination unit.

Marc followed until they were safely in the unit. When they shut the door, he moved back down the hallway toward the front of the facility. When he passed the residence area, he moved carefully. He checked each turn in the hall before he exposed himself to hostiles.

So far, so good.

He reached the third airlock from the residence area and spotted the hallway with a black phenolic sign above a door that indicated Dr. von Wirth's office. He counted the doors and moved.

He hit the door on the fly and it gave way. He burst into the room and a shooter came around with a pistol. Marc unleashed a burst of 9mm death pellets from the Uzi and the shooter crumpled.

There were two people, both women, in the room. "Please don't shoot us," one woman cried. "Haven't you people done enough?"

"I'm not going to hurt you. I'm here to get you out. Explanations come later. Now, let's go," Marc said.

The women looked stunned and puzzled for a long moment.

"Let's go now, ladies!" Marc said firmly.

The women were up and moving toward the door when Marc turned around. A man with a rifle appeared and opened his mouth to sound a warning when Marc dispatched him with a double three-round burst. The guy fell back and slammed into the wall.

"Go to Decontamination Unit One. Run as hard as you can and stay close with me."

The women nodded.

Marc led the way. He hit the hallway on the run, the women behind him. They were near the first turn in the hallway when a shot rang out behind them. One of the women stumbled, but she didn't fall.

Marc dropped low and fired a long burst with the sound-suppressed subgun. The shooter took the flying death pellets in the chest and slammed into the wall. Blood splattered wildly and covered the floor and walls around him. He fell dead without another shot.

Marc grabbed the wounded woman around the arm and helped her run through the hallway. "You'll be all right. If it'll make you feel better, my name's Marc."

"I'm Cathy and I think you're an angel."

Marc forced a smile. "Well, Cathy, there are some people who would probably argue with you on that one. Keep moving."

They reached the decontamination unit and opened the door.

More shots rang out. Shooters came from both directions now.

Marc shoved the women inside and opened fire. He dropped to his knees. A shooter to the left sent lead death into the doorway above his head. He spun and fired the Uzi into the guy's face. The shooter toppled backward amidst spraying blood and painful screams.

Another shooter was on the right now. He fired an

assault rifle. The projectiles bounced off of the hard walls and landed into the ceiling without causing harm.

Marc dropped the empty stick from the Uzi and slammed another one up the well. He spun around toward the shooter and fired a long burst.

The shooter appeared stunned and then he fell dead.

Marc closed the door and slammed the security latch closed from the inside. "Okay, ladies. Up into the overhead tunnel and out into the containment unit. Go to the back and crawl through the airlock door. Turn left and run to the ladder. I'll meet you there."

The women obeyed and disappeared into the overhead tunnel. Marc made a tactical magazine change in the Uzi and followed the ladies.

They reached the other side and crawled into the airlock. Behind them, a man was beating on the window to the containment unit. Cathy turned around and glanced over her shoulder. "'Bye, Jon," she yelled, and then she crawled through the airlock.

Marc worked the switches on two more DFC-2 charges and tossed them toward the front windows of the Containment Unit. "So that's Jon," he said aloud. "He doesn't look too tough to me right now."

Jon stood wide-eyed and stared at the explosives on the other side of the heavy glass. He watched while Marc disappeared through the wall at the back of the room.

Marc secured the outer security latch on the airlock door and moved toward the ladder. He got there and the first woman climbed up. Marc grabbed Cathy and helped her on the first rung. "It's a long climb, can you do it?"

"Damn right," Cathy said. "Let's do it and get out of this hellhole."

Several minutes passed and they reached the top. Marc pushed Cathy ahead into Carl's waiting arms. He looked around when he climbed from the hole. A half-dozen concrete trucks sat parked in a spokelike circle with their chutes aimed at the hole. "Let it go," Marc said. "Fill that son of a bitch up."

Dr. Caldwell came running forward. She grabbed Marc and squeezed him tightly. "You did it. By God, you did it!"

Marc smiled. "How about the elevator shaft, Major?"

"Five more trucks over there dumping right now. This place is sealed forever. And by the way, Colonel, NASA launched the shuttle fifteen minutes ago. Thought you'd like to know," Carl said.

Marc's face was blank. "Bastards," he said. "We were just a diversion."

Dr. Caldwell looked at Marc and then Carl. "I don't know what you're talking about, but thank you. Both of you. And thank God this horror is over."

The ground rumbled and vibrated without warning when the timed charges left by Marc detonated beneath the earth. And the chemical and bacteriological horror that resided beneath the ground at Huntsville became an inferno of cleansing hellfire sealed forever under tons of fresh concrete.

Marc and Carl stood beside the Leeco rig outside the FBI office in Huntsville. Dr. Caldwell and Agent Hargrove shook their hands and bade them good-bye.

Hargrove looked over the Leeco rig. "I've never seen anything like this machine. It's spectacular."

"Yeah, it is one of a kind." Carl chuckled.

"So you found Senator Whitten?" Marc said.

"Yes," Hargrove said. "Two agents found him hanging around beneath the deck of his home on Kentucky Lake in southern Kentucky. He left a detailed and documented suicide letter. He told it all. He and Ashland had funneled funds into the laboratory and Dr. von Wirth for years. Ashland hired the Central American mercenaries to help some of his drivers get control of Marshall and the lab. They wanted to take all of the weapons and use them as bargaining chips in an elaborate financial scheme with an undisclosed Arab state. They left a vicious web and Dr. von Wirth was tricked into thinking he was moving to another laboratory. Nonetheless, he was dirty, too. Whitten got nervous and tipped the Bureau on the reactor scheme. He planned to take the chemicals for himself and cut the deal. He burned Ashland, but the web snared him, too."

"Damn," Marc said. "What about the nuclear reactor we were hauling?"

Hargrove laughed. "You had a decoy. It was worthless and totally nonfunctional. The real one was shipped by Federal Express four days ago."

"What was Ashland's involvement with the shuttle?" Dr. Caldwell asked.

"He planned to load some of the weapons into the shuttle in the cavities of its engines. Huntsville was the place for that. He also planned to stow some of it away in the cargo, but he didn't get it out of here in time. Thank God," Hargrove said.

"At least they didn't get any of the weapons out of the facility," Dr. Caldwell said.

"Right," Carl said. "They had everything at the last airlock to be loaded on the truck. It's under six feet of concrete right now."

"Where do you guys go from here?" Dr. Caldwell asked, looking at Marc longingly.

Marc returned the affectionate look. "I guess that's up to the Jons, the Ashlands, and the Montinos of the world. We'll go find some more misguided souls like them and see if we can cause them to have nightmares."

## ACTION ON EIGHTEEN WHEELS!

When a fanatical band of terrorists hijack an ultra-deadly cache of nuclear weapons, Marc Lee and Carl Browne—ex–Delta Force warriors and now the men of Overload—find themselves tackling their most dangerous mission yet: locating the arsenal buried near Lake Michigan and blasting the kill-crazy fanatics straight into hell before they can unleash wholesale devastation on the Midwest!

Here's an exciting preview of Book #10 in Bob Ham's OVERLOAD series:

# MICHIGAN MADNESS

*Coming in April 1991, wherever Bantam Books are sold.*

# Chapter One

□ □ □

*Tuesday Morning*

Something just didn't feel right, but Carney Putnam didn't know exactly what it was, couldn't put his finger on it. But one thing he did know, the fog and the cool breeze drifting across Lake Michigan left him with an eerie sensation. There was something about it he couldn't explain, but his gut instincts were screaming at him and telling him to step up the caution level. Even if just a little.

He'd spent thirty-five years running cargo across the broad inland expanse of water and he knew when the environment didn't feel the way it was supposed to. Maybe it was because he always worried when he carried the plutonium for the government.

And this was one of those nights.

The old tub, as he called the *Polly P*, creaked and groaned as it plowed north against a head wind on the giant open body of fresh water. The diesel engines belowdeck of the big freighter hummed a dull, boring tune as they sent the power to turn the twin screws beneath the water in sync. The repetitious clanking of the cams and the hum of the radar antenna rotating overhead at the bridge was sufficiently monotonous in itself to cause even an energetic man to go to sleep.

At three in the morning, Carney felt anything but energetic. And right now, he wanted to go to sleep. Actually, he wanted to go below to his modest captain's quarters, sip a glass of brandy, kick his boots off, smoke a stogie, and relax in his bunk until the roll of the waves against the bow caused him to drift off into restful sleep.

But there could be no sleep tonight. Not with three of his regular ten-man crew out with some gut-wrenching viral infection. There was too much to do and too few hours to do it. Bilge was becoming a problem and Carney knew he had to replace the pumps when they docked at Bay City. The three replacements he'd hustled from a bar on the docks at Milwaukee were working out okay, but they didn't know the ropes. By the time they learned to do things the way he liked them done, the regulars would be back. At least, so he hoped.

Gurley Galopagus opened the rickety door to the bridge and walked in. "'Mornin', Cap'n. A damn-sight bone chilling out there this morn'n, hey?"

"Aye, Gurley. I was just thinking to myself that this night ain't feelin' quite right. Maybe it's the fog. Fog does that to your senses, you know," Putnam said. "I recall once on a troop transport ship back during the Big War we got ourselves swallowed up in the fog. It'll have you barking up your own ass before you know it."

Gurley laughed. "Aye, Cap'n, maybe that's it. Maybe the fog has us all chasin' our tails. What's weather like ahead?"

"Clearing by mornin', winds out of the north at fifteen knots. More of that arctic blast headed our way. Gets nippy when the north wind blows," Putnam said. He made a slight adjustment in the freighter's course and checked his wheel movement against the big black and white compass mounted between him and the forward glass. "Fog doesn't bother me as much as runnin' through these shallows. Even with radar and the depth sounder, it still makes my skin tingle sometimes."

"Can't say I won't welcome it, the northern that is. Maybe it'll blow this fog out of here. I can't seem to figger why the shallows bother you, Cap'n. You've shot 'em a thousand times."

"And it's tingled my skin a thousand times, Gurley."

"It's a long way to Bay City. Goin' around the point at the peninsula might get a little on the frigid side with the northern blowin' in. Hey, but what the hell, huh? That's why we got them heaters down below. Am I right, Cap'n?"

Putnam laughed. "Right as usual, Gurley."

The rig shook with a resounding vibration followed an instant later by the roar of an explosion. Almost before the vibration stopped and the roar died away, the *Polly P* listed hard to the starboard.

When Putnam and Gurley regained their balance, both of their scraggly-looking faces were pale. "What the hell was it, Cap'n?" Gurley yelled.

Blood trickled down Putnam's face. He fought to stand and held tightly to the wheel. He looked aft and saw towers of black smoke funneling toward the sky. "Gurley, get us a damage report. We've blown somewhere. Intercom's dead."

Gurley forced himself to walk against the list and moved toward the door.

It swung open and a man dressed in solid black stood there. His face was cold and brutal. And in his hands there was a .45 automatic. "Not a good night to be out of doors, mate."

Gurley froze.

Putnam looked through weakening eyes at the figure holding the gun. "What the hell is this?"

"Deep six," the man's cold voice answered. He lifted the .45 on line and fired three shots into Gurley's face.

Gurley slumped backward and blood splayed on the air and filled the cabin with crimson-red death.

Putnam leapt for the window, but three more messengers of death flew from the bore of the smoking .45. They ate through his flesh like enraged and starving barracudas shooting through a school of shad. And when their energy was spent, Putnam's life drifted away into the dark fog and left him lying in a drifting sea of blood.

The *Polly P* rolled hard to starboard now and her stern swallowed up the water of the Great Lake. Another explosion vibrated through her dying carcass. In minutes, her bow lifted out of the water and she sank to the dark sandy bottom below.

*Wednesday Morning*

Marc Lee crouched in the scrubby underbrush and scanned the terminal with his rubber-armored binoculars. He could see them in the light of the mercury-vapor lights, men in camouflaged field dress, milling around all three buildings within the fenced compound below. He spoke softly into the throat microphone of the tactical radio harness connected to his Icom U-16 transceiver. "I count eighteen men and seven rigs. How's the total from your angle?"

Carl Browne spoke softly also. He crouched in the darkness a hundred yards west of Marc and watched the movement in the compound. "I got the same count. We do it by the numbers?"

"Is there any other way?" Marc asked. He knew before he said it that his partner would call the play the same way he did. The Delta Force Warriors turned Highway Warriors had been together far too long for it to go any other way—from their meeting in military basic training, to their camaraderie in Delta Force, up to the present, when they were fighting in another kind of never-ending war—this one on the soil of the very country they had fought to preserve on all too many blood-soaked foreign soils.

"Negative," Carl replied. He made a touch check of his arms and accessories. The Beretta 9mm was snug in the shoulder leather under his left arm. The Smith & Wesson rode comfortably on his hip in the Uncle Mike's nylon rig. He slid the Smith from its sheath and checked the magazine. He knew it was full, but it was a common practice he had developed many years ago . . . a result of field-honed survival strategies etched in his mind from bloody battles on the killing fields of a world gone mad. Satisfied with the Smith, Carl checked the Beretta to reassure himself. With the hammer drops thumbed up on both auto pistols, they were ready for instant duty, should the situation arise, in the war of cleansing hellfire. Then he dropped the thirty-round magazine from the Delta HBAR M-16/A2. He pressed the top round of SS109 ammo to be sure the stick was filled to capacity. It was. He shoved the Colt aluminum mag back into the well and slapped it home. He heard the familiar and reassuring click. Then he pulled the charging lever all the way to the rear and let it slam closed, taking with it the first round from the top of the thirty-rounder. He slid the sound-suppressed Uzi from his shoulder, dropped the stick from its well, and made the obligatory mag check. Then he slid the little subgun back on his shoulder on its sling. An experimentally modified LAW disposable rocket-launcher tube was strung across his back on its sling. He carried the fragmentation projectiles for the tube in his oversized fanny pack. A couple of CS gas grenades and a half-dozen fragmentation grenades completed his belt arsenal. His trusted Parker-Imai K-632 fighting knife rode low on his left hip.

Marc made his own mind-easing weapons check. He, too, carried a Colt Delta HBAR M-16/A2 in 5.56mm and a sound-suppressed Uzi chambered for 9mm Parabellum. But rather than a LAW tube, he carried an experimental laser sighting device similar in size to an old .30-caliber M-1 Carbine. The little Zytel-stocked field piece could shoot a beam of invisible light for at least a thousand yards. The beam, in itself, was harmless, but it paved the way to awesome destruction for the also-experimental laser-guided missiles Carl carried in addition to the frag rounds for the LAW. Carl's tube had been modified for feed-fire with the fiberglass high-tech guided explosive. When the laser sight aligned on the target, Carl could finger a lightning-fast missile. The new explosive round was designated DFEP-Hellfire for Delta Force Experimental Portable Hellfire.

The trucking terminal below them inside the security fence was a front. A living, functional contradiction. The men in camos weren't everyday truckers either. They were a cell of highly trained renegade gunmen who were bent on the disruption of normal civilization . . . terrorists. American terrorists. Guns for hire to the highest bidder, damn the cause and to hell with the reason. They were misguided souls who had made the wrong choices for their lives. And now those inaccurate choices were about to cause the ultimate debt to be collected. Cleansing fire sat just 150 yards away cradled in the arms of Marc Lee and Carl Browne. The mighty eagle of undiluted justice was poised, its dark wings taut, ready to swoop down and pluck the doers of heinous savagery from the bowels of the very society that was the object of their misguided wrath.

Marc finished his weapons check and lifted the binoculars to his face for one more satisfying look before he unleashed scorching hellfire on the ground where the doers of evil stood. He spoke into the VOX microphone unit once more. "Five seconds on my mark, Major. Five, four, three, two, one. Let's party!"

Carl was up and running with the count. He moved forward stealthily in a crouch, the Delta HBAR poised in his hands and ready to breathe scorching death. He kept his eyes fixed on the area where the men in camo fatigues moved around, oblivious to the attack about to devour them. Carl glanced only once to his right, into the darkness, where he knew Marc would be moving also. He caressed the HBAR's trigger like a mother clinging to her newborn baby. It took twenty seconds for him to reach the outer security fence. Then he stopped, removed a pair of heavy bolt cutters from his musette bag, and clipped a hole in the diamond-patterned fencing. That done, he dropped the cutters back into the pack, slid the LAW tube from his back, and dropped to his knees.

Marc was five seconds behind Carl. He worked around to the east until he reached the area he had chosen for his entry into the highly secure compound. Like Carl, he clipped a hole in the fencing, peeled back the heavy wire, and slid the carbine-style electronic sight from his shoulder. He chose the larger of the three buildings and aimed the laser into a huge overhead garage door. "Beacon's burning. Give 'em Hellfire."

Carl slid a fiberglass rocket into the tube until it touched home. He aimed in the direction of the huge door and touched off the missile. A resounding whoosh echoed through the night. The experimental Hellfire-style missile shot from the tube and streaked across the night toward the door. Midway between the fence and the tube, the rocket corrected its course and homed in on the invisible laser beam poised on the building door.

In the time it took the camo-clad men to react to the whoosh sound, the experimental rocket made contact with the door. The early-morning sky lit up brightly from the intensity of the explosion. An orange fireball shot skyward. The concussion from the explosion rolled across the paved lot like a cyclonic whirlwind, knocking the camo men to the ground before they could move.

Marc slung the laser sight device over his shoulder and moved at the sound of the whoosh. Heat from the intensely burning fire at the largest of the three buildings seared the pavement, but Marc zigzagged across the lot. He held the Delta HBAR M-16 by the pistol grip with his right hand. His index finger was threaded through the trigger guard and ready to twitch sizzling death in the blink of an eye.

Carl slung the disposable tube over his shoulder and moved out also. He ran across the lot and stopped in the cover of one of the buildings adjacent to the one now on fire. He dropped to one knee and shouldered the Delta HBAR. He leveled the sight on one of the camo-clad men who was struggling to get up from the ground and unsheathe an automatic pistol from a holster on his hip. Carl let the guy clear leather and search the fence line with the muzzle of the weapon. When the pistol-wielding man finally stood, Carl tapped out a three-round burst of sizzling death.

The shooter took all three rounds in the chest and pivoted back to the ground. Other men scrambled to their feet now, drawing weapons as they scurried for cover. Carl laid the sights on another one and tapped off his second three-round burst. The shooter took the death staccato in the neck and spiraled backward into eternity.

Shots were coming from inside the building nearest Marc on the opposite side of the burning building. Shooters fired into the darkness without finding a target. The lot and the buildings were consumed with fire and chaos now. Men were moving erratically and searching for cover from the unseen death menace descending upon them from the darkness.

Marc found two camo-clad citizens crouched behind a line of fifty-five-gallon barrels. He watched them for a minute while they searched the opposite end of the lot for the source of the hellstorm. He strained hard to read the white labeling on the barrels. It was difficult, but he finally read VARSOL. "Bingo," he mumbled. He reached to his utility belt and retrieved a hand grenade. He held the spoon tightly against the body and pulled the pin free. Then he tossed the grenade with pinpoint precision between the wall of the building and the barrels.

The men jerked around and searched the darkness for the source of the loud cracking thud emitted when the grenade struck the pavement. By the time they found it, it was far too late. He heard one man yell "Grenade," an instant before the pineapple exploded. The guy's frantic cry was lost in the shattering explosion when the fire from the grenade ignited the barrels of Varsol. The ground shook and more fire joined the flaming towers already belching from the burning building. The explosion lifted the men from the ground and sent them sailing in the air. Their flight ended when their flaming, lifeless torsos slapped into the pavement and rolled to a stop.

Men ran from the other two buildings now, their weapons chattering a full-auto death chant into unseen targets hidden from their view in the darkness.

Marc and Carl had them trapped in a cross fire. The Highway Warriors were both down on one knee, their Delta HBARs shouldered. In unison, both of the heavy-barreled M-16s spat super-stabilized SS109 full-metal-jacketed hornets at the shooters. The lead-core copper-jacketed projectiles spiraled through flesh and sent a misty sea of blood spraying into the air in their wake. The shooters fell to the blood-soaked pavement like dominoes as Marc and Carl cleansed the lot with sanitizing hellfire.

Another wave of shooters emerged from the burning building and the one nearest Carl. Every man who came into view was armed and firing wildly. Carl picked the one nearest him and sent a staccato of death singing an eternal death chant into the man's chest. The shooter stopped all forward momentum and fell to the scorching pavement.

Marc saw three men running across the lot toward one of the five eighteen-wheelers parked in the shadows at the opposite side of the lot. He trained the sight of the Delta HBAR on them and unleased a burst of 5.56mm justice. The shooters took the hits and fell lifelessly to the pavement before their bodies could take another step.

The fire at the first building had spread to the one nearest Marc with the assistance of the Varsol petroleum-cleaning solvent that had exploded from the grenade Marc had sent sailing. The sky lit orange red and cyclonic towers of fiery smoke shot into the atmosphere. There were screams of confusion from inside the building. And behind it, the roar of a diesel engine starting caught Marc's attention. He spoke into the microphone. "We got a rabbit out back. When he clears the building, I'll drop the dot on him and see if you can send a bird up his ass."

"Roger," Carl replied. He laid the Delta HBAR across his lap and grabbed for the DFEP tube. He shuffled around and retrieved a rocket from the fanny pack, slid it into the tube, and cradled the trigger. "I'm ready, Colonel."

The fleeing eighteen-wheeler appeared at the corner of the building and sped across the lot toward the locked gates at the end opposite Marc's position. Marc laid the invisible sight on the fuel tanks and peeped through the electronic sight to see where the magic dot fell. "Now!" he said into the throat mike.

Carl aimed in the general direction of the truck and touched the firing trigger. Another whoosh spat from the tube and sent a roaring thunderbolt toward the fleeing rig. The electronic homing device on the nose of the fiberglass projectile found the source it sought and crashed into the rig's fuel tanks with an earth-shattering explosion. The rig listed to one side, rocked hard, and burst into fiery fragments amid a scorching cataclysmic fireball.

"Good shootin', Major," Marc said. "You sure took

the wind out of his sails. Let's move in on 'em and mop this up."

"Affirmative," Carl replied. He slung the tube over his shoulder and cradled the Delta HBAR. He moved forward against a hailstorm of death pellets that sailed erratically into the darkness. He ran a zigzag pattern and the mighty A2 sent swarms of killer hornets into the remaining hardcases.

Marc did likewise. He was up and running into the lighted area of the lot before the men trapped by chaos spotted him. He screamed at them: "Drop your weapons and lie on the pavement."

His command was met with automatic-weapons fire when the camo-clad hardcases spun around. Marc dropped prone and spent the remainder of his thirty-round magazine into them. He made a fast move to get to another stick, but there wasn't time. He drew the Smith & Wesson 5906 9mm from his hip holster and fired the first round double action into a shooter who fingered the trigger on an Ingram MAC-10. The first round struck the man in the upper chest and then two more fast semiauto shots tore through his midsection. The shooter flung the Ingram wildly and twisted to the pavement.

Marc grabbed another thirty-round stick from his musette bag and slapped it up the well of the HBAR. He pressed the bolt release and the heavy spring slapped the bolt shut while it stripped the first round from the top of the stick. He moved out now, all of the visible shooters down. He went to the building nearest him and kicked the door open. He swept the inside with the muzzle of the HBAR and found nothing. He moved through the building carefully, checking each small room and doorway before he entered. Then he reached the warehouse section and kicked the door open. Smoke belched out at him followed immediately by heavy gunfire from a pair of hidden shooters. Marc assessed the situation, returned a short burst of autofire, and lifted a fragmentation grenade from his belt. He jerked the pin free and tossed the hand bomb toward the gunfire. Then he ducked out into the hallway and hit the floor. A loud explosion preceded screams of agonizing death as the two shooters met eternity. Marc rushed into the warehouse room and searched for survivors.

He found none.

Carl entered the building he had used seconds earlier for cover. He searched for a target with the sweeping barrel of the HBAR, but there was none visible. He did a room-by-room search. He reached a barricaded room near the back. There was a heavy lock dangling from the door. He moved the door open slowly and fired a burst of hellfire into the room.

There was no reply.

Carl rushed into the room and stopped cold. There on the floor lay the brutalized body of Bernie Compton . . . silent and dead. Beside Compton's body were a dozen empty wooden crates with distinct military markings and encoding. Carl spoke into the microphone. "I got Compton and the goods," he said.

"Roger. It's clean over on this end. Where are you?"

"First building on the end. You comin'?"

"Yeah," Marc replied. "On my way. How's Compton?"

"Stone-cold dead," Carl replied. "All the crates are empty, too."

"Wonderful," Marc replied. In seconds he had worked his way to the building where Carl stood staring at Compton's body.

"Nice touch, huh?" Carl said as he stared at Compton's lifeless form on the floor. The guy's throat was slit from ear to ear and his tongue protruded through the opening and dangled from the place where his Adam's apple should have been. "A damned Colombian necktie. These people are barbarians."

"Yeah," Marc replied as he felt the gastric juices churning in his stomach. "And the hell of it is, they've got a dozen experimental low-yield personal nuclear-rocket tubes. And God only knows how much ammo they've pilfered to go with it."

"Yeah," Carl said. "Compton gave his life to get these bastards and look at him now. We've got to find Tommy Dominick before they find out how to make more missiles for these things."

"All they need is plutonium and some ingenuity and we've got a serious problem on our hands," Marc replied. "Tommy Dominick's middle name is madness. Compton is evidence to that."

Carl nodded in agreement and then both Warriors spun around in unison when they heard the footsteps coming behind them.

# *Action on Eighteen Wheels!*

Marc Lee and Carl Browne, ex-Delta Force anti-terrorist commandos: They've taken on bloodthirsty Middle Eastern terrorists...deadly drug cartels...vicious bikers...the Mafia...no matter how badly they're outnumbered, Lee and Browne always come up swinging...and blasting!

Don't miss any of the exciting books in Bob Ham's OVERLOAD SERIES!